I0642275

Bonamy Price, Michel Chevalier

The principles of currency

Six lectures delivered at Oxford

Bonamy Price, Michel Chevalier

The principles of currency
Six lectures delivered at Oxford

ISBN/EAN: 9783742811608

Manufactured in Europe, USA, Canada, Australia, Japa

Cover: Foto ©Andreas Hilbeck / pixelio.de

Manufactured and distributed by brebook publishing software
(www.brebook.com)

Bonamy Price, Michel Chevalier

The principles of currency

PREFACE.

The following Lectures were delivered as Public Lectures at Oxford in the Taylor Institution through the kindness of its Curators. Some apology is due for the repetitions which occur in them. I can only plead with Bastiat that *Bis repetita docent.* In the present state of men's minds about currency, the constant recourse to fundamental principles at each point of their application is almost a necessity.

M. Michel Chevalier's Letter has laid me under heavy obligations to that great Economist. It contains the record of a service rendered to a whole people immeasurably more beneficial, more deserving of its gratitude, than most of the triumphs of war or politics.

I have to thank Mr. Charles Gairdner, the Manager of the Union Bank of Scotland at Glasgow, for his admirable Paper of Answers to the Questions addressed to him by the Imperial Commission of France.

The Athenæum. *Jan.* 12. 1860.

CONTENTS.

viii   *Contents.*

APPENDIX I.

APPENDIX II.

APPENDIX III.

LECTURE I.

POLITICAL Economy, in respect of the range of its subject-matter, has no superior, if indeed it has an equal, amongst the sciences. It treats of wealth, of its production and of its distribution, and the larger part of human life is spent in the exercise of these two functions. Political Economy is often spoken of as a modern science: but it has existed in all ages, and amongst all civilized nations. Men at all times have occupied themselves with the creation of wealth according to certain rules and ideas : for no laborious employment can be extensively carried on without the existence of some notions as to the right way of working, and the most fitting methods for attaining the end desired. It is a mistake, though a very common one, to suppose that practical men, as they are called, are destitute of theory. The exact reverse of this statement is true. Practical men swarm with theories, none more so. They abound in views, in ideas, in rules which they endow with the pompous authority of experience : and when new principles

B

are proposed, none are so quick as practical men to
overwhelm the innovator with an army of the wisdom
which is to be found in prevalent practice. I know
of no place which is so entirely under the dominion
of loudly-asserted theories as the City. In some
departments of Political Economy, the doctrines of
merchants and bankers have subdued the whole land,
and almost put a stop to all independent thought
which should presume to contradict the established
theories of men of business. Adam Smith's illustrious work is almost wholly devoted to the demolition
of the huge superstructure of doctrine which traders
had reared up on their practice. The difference which
separates the man of science from the man of practice does not consist in the presence of general views
and ideas on one side, and their absence on the other.
Both have views and ideas. The distinction lies in
the method by which those views have been reached,
in the breadth and completeness of the investigation
pursued, in the rigorous questioning of facts, and the
careful digestion of the instruction they contain, in
the co-ordination and the logical cohesion of the
truths established.

No science has suffered so severely at the hands
of practical and empirical men as Political Economy.
They have at all times propounded and acted on doctrines of the most elaborate kind. The more directly
engaged in business was the speaker, the more complicated, the more artificial, the more mysterious
have been the rules he laid down for the attainment
of wealth. Monopolies were proclaimed to be the
infallible means for securing good and trustworthy
quality in manufacture. Guilds were invented for
the right regulation of the relations between master

and scholar, between capital and labour. A complex organization was created for the enrolment and in-struction of apprentices : and if ever a human system was founded on elaborate theory, it was the insti-tution of guilds. Then, again, when the discovery of the New World enlarged geography with colonies of a novel kind, the practical man speedily stepped forward with his theory, and taught the statesman that the secret of the new and boundless wealth en-gendered by colonies lay in the exclusive appro-priation of their trade by the mother-country. His teaching was adopted by every civilized country, and became the recognized policy of all Europe. Great wars were waged in the name of the practical man's ideas : his views were supreme over all colonial relations. His doctrines were strong enough to put fetters on the trade of Ireland, and to command the out-flow of her productions to be directed upon England ; and these were doctrines, not worked out by careful analysis and accurate reasoning, but roughly gathered from the first crude thoughts suggested by the outward appearance of trade. The practical man's ascendency thus rose ever higher and higher, till it reached its culminating point in the famed mercantile theory, the final development of com-mercial thought, the crowning embodiment of the wisdom which practical prudence and experience had inspired. The precious metals were held up as the one supreme object of industrial ambition. To ac-quire them, to apply the resources of the intellect, the capital, and the labour of a nation to their acqui-sition, to exalt the export over the import trade, as attracting homewards the inflow of the wealth-im-parting stream of metal, to be ever selling and never

buying, and to measure national prosperity by the
tale of accumulated ingots,—were pressed by practical men on prince and peasant, on merchant and
tradesman, as the highest aim of human efforts, and
the surest counsel of human wisdom.

Theory, then, is inevitable. There always has
been, and there always will be, theory taking upon
itself to guide practice on a matter of such profound
interest as the acquirement of wealth. One of two
things is absolutely certain to occupy the seat of
authority, the theory of the practical man or the
theory of the man of science. Men must be Political
Economists. You may not, individually, be merchants
or Members of Parliament or clergymen or land-
owners, but Political Economists, one and all of you,
you cannot help being. You will have ideas, each
of you, on Political Economy, which will act on the
world around you; and, most assuredly, during the
whole of your lives, and wherever you may be
placed, you will be reacted on by the ideas of others
on Political Economy. Your own fortunes and the
fortunes of your neighbours and connexions will be
affected, for better or for worse, by the views which
will prevail on Political Economy: for those views
will influence alike, over a vast range of human
existence, the legislation of the country and the
conduct of private citizens. Every one in this room
has been made the richer or the poorer by the doctrines which have governed the practice of Political
Economy in the past; and the actual state of the
world abundantly shows that the final triumph of
not one of these doctrines has yet been achieved, and
that, before your respective careers are ended, the
state of your incomes may bear witness to changes of

Economical legislation which may have enriched or impoverished you.

But there are other and nobler motives, besides personal loss and gain, which invite you to the study of Political Economy. The power and prosperity of your country, the well-being of its population, their sense of the justice of its legislation, and their contentment with the social order that surrounds them, are largely involved in a correct apprehension and a firm application of the teaching of this science. You belong to the classes which enjoy the largest leisure for study ; you fill positions in life which command the greatest number of hearers, and furnish the widest opportunities for exercising influence. I am not exaggerating the importance of the science which it is my duty to explain, when I affirm that, if you leave Oxford with a clear perception and an effectual mastery of its principles, you will have acquired great power for successfully filling any position to which you may hereafter be called. Your efficiency, your command over the varied elements of modern civilization, your ability to take part in the movements of the world, in its debates and its practice, will be enormously increased. The need for good Political Economy will meet you at every turn, in public or private discussions, in meetings of every kind, in the solemn debates of Parliament. The demand for the counsels of Political Economy will be as varied as it will be large. Think of the history of your country during the last forty years, and you will see how vast a portion of its public life has hinged on Political Economy. No question, except perhaps the peculiarly exciting topic of Reform, has rivalled in public interest the great

question of Free Trade. The agitation raised on
the laws which governed the importation of food
long convulsed every portion of English society.
It was a battle which raged upon a doctrine of
science. The struggle for the repeal of the Corn
Laws cost seven campaigns to one of the most
eminent of English statesmen, and its result infinitely transcended in world-wide importance the
effect of the famous war of the great Prussian King.
It stormed with the angriest passions and the
fiercest animosities. The most numerous and the
richest classes in the country alike believed that
their property—nay, that their very existence—was
at stake, and the fury with which they fought was
proportionate to the strength of the conviction.
And yet the question at issue was one of pure
science and reasoning. Its decision belonged of
right to Political Economy, to the students who had
mastered its principles, and could predict consequences with the authority of cultivated intelligence.
But, unfortunately, neither people nor Parliament
had yet thoroughly apprehended the teaching of this
most practical of sciences. The agricultural classes
trembled at the impending cessation of English
tillage; their wheat-lands were speedily to become
wastes. Nevertheless, reason and argument ultimately prevailed, but at the cost of the overthrow
of one of the strongest governments of modern times.
A great minister fell because he was a Political
Economist, and his followers were not. Sir Robert
Peel was driven from power for an illustrious act,
performed in the name of true science, because he
was scientifically in advance of his party. The
ignorance which then prevailed on Political Economy

disorganized the political world, and its consequences are felt up to this very hour.

But it is not Parliamentary politicians alone whose fame and whose power have hung upon the hold which they had of Political Economy. Mighty sovereigns also have devoted their minds to the study of its truths, and have applied them in practice with conspicuous benefit to their subjects, and immense glory to themselves. The celebrated session of the English Parliament in 1860 found the subject-matter of its vehement debates in the enlightenment of an Emperor by the instructions of a teacher of Political Economy. That teacher was Mr. Cobden, and that pupil the Emperor Napoleon. Mr. Cobden preached Free Trade, its life-giving power, its prodigious energy in developing the industry of a nation, and the splendour of its results. The Emperor heard and was convinced: and the nature of his position enabled him to secure at once for France some of the benefits which his education in Political Economy had taught him to perceive. He became a Political Economist: but he was almost a solitary convert amidst a nation profoundly hostile to the science. It did not cost him a seven years' war to give effect to his scientific principles. He was an absolute sovereign, and he availed himself of his political power to benefit his people in spite of themselves. As sovereign, he signed a Reciprocity Treaty with England, which even his influence might have failed to pass successfully through the Chambers : and thus, by his own personal act, he abolished prohibition — that contradictory of Free Trade — which disgraced the Statute-book of France. He invited the aid. of England in the accomplishment of this beneficent

task by revising her tariff on French wines: and
the two forces combined, the French Emperor and
the English Parliament, reconstructed the principles
of the commercial legislation of France. It was a
noble triumph of science, the more glorious, because
it furnished a striking example of how Political
Economy not only blessed the people which practised
it, but built up mutual good-will amongst the various
nations of the world by the good which its teaching
enabled them to do to each other.

Free Trade is not the only question on which
Political Economy offers a field for the application
of sound knowledge, and the realization of its resulting advantages. There are many subjects still open
for settlement. Political Economy has not yet taken
its departure from the House of Commons. Some of
you will probably be enrolled amongst its members;
you will assuredly find that the demand for the
teaching of this science will daily become more
urgent, and that the influence of those who are most
thoroughly impregnated with its spirit will ever rise
higher and higher in general estimation. Taxation
in all its forms, its incidence, its equality, and its
productiveness, the expediency and the limits of
Government intervention in commercial matters, the
machinery of public and private finance, the laws of
partnership and limited liability, the relations of
capital to labour, have laid hold of the national mind,
and must engage the attention of every man who
takes a part in public affairs. As soon as you leave
the University you will find these subjects occupying
a large position in your daily life. If you engage in
any of the manifold pursuits of commerce, as agri-
culturists, or merchants, or bankers, you will be

assailed by strongly-expressed ideas on the conduct
of these matters; you will be called upon for
opinions, and for advice as to courses to be pursued,
not only by those with whom you will come in
contact, but still more by your own minds. You
will feel the need of light to guide you: for it
is daily more difficult in England to float along the
stream of life at hap-hazard, and to take no thought
for guiding conduct by attainment. Nor will such
of you as become clergymen escape the necessity of
being Political Economists. Not only will your
incomes be closely connected with the successful
cultivation of the land, but your higher respon-
sibilities also will be constantly urging you to re-
flect on the social links which connect together the
various classes of your people; claims will constantly
present themselves of economical good and of justice
to be carried out, of which you ought to be the
intelligent and persistent advocates. Good left un-
done, and evil acquiesced in, from carelessness, are
amongst the most fruitful causes of human suffering: and who has so many opportunities for wit-
nessing the action of these causes as the parochial
clergyman? At the same time, it may not be im-
proper to remind you that the very consciousness
of his high mission to combat evil and relieve suffering may lay dangerous snares for the clergyman.
Philanthropy without knowledge is not the least
dangerous of errors. Society has not seldom had
to lament the effects of zealous, but unintelligent,
benevolence. It is almost as easy to injure as to
benefit the poor by measures which have their origin
in the purest desire to promote their welfare. Evils
which are invisible in a single cottage often reveal

themselves with calamitous power amidst numbers:
and the clergyman, whose sphere of action is limited
to the area of a parish in a country of such mobility
as modern England, needs to understand the laws of
social aggregation.   Political Economy, therefore, for
him is no strange or profane science.   He must, as
I have said already, be a Political Economist of some
kind : it is no light matter whether he adopts his
principles without reflection, or whether he learns
to distinguish between the false and the true.   At
this very moment we hear the cry often raised that
the wealth of the nation is the exclusive product of
those who work with manual labour, and invests
them with claims for consideration and reward to
which no other class in the community has a title.
It is not difficult to imagine the feelings which such
language is calculated to suggest, when addressed to
large and excited masses,—what pretensions it may
raise to a new distribution of the fruits of industry.
Who have such fair opportunities for combating this
unjust and unfounded assumption as the parochial
clergy over the whole land ?   Who possess such easy
access to the minds of the working-men, and can
explain, with so much advantage and so much
authority, the part which the thinker, the man of
science, the capitalist, and the organizer, take in
giving efficiency and success to labour ?   And if the
clergyman possesses peculiar means for diffusing this
healing instruction, does he not lie under the
strongest obligation to learn how to perform this
great function well ?

I might go through other stations in society which
some of you in the course of years will naturally be
called to fill, and illustrate in each case the presence

of the same law and of the same duty. But I have
said enough to show the vast space which the subject
of which Political Economy treats now occupies in
civilized life. You have seen that ideas and theories
will always be proclaimed as to the fitting methods
for creating and distributing wealth; and you will
have gathered, I trust, how universally it concerns
the whole nation and every individual member of it
that these ideas should be correct, that these theories
should be true; and that a matter constituting so
incomparably the largest part of human life should
be guided by right principle. Political Economy
invites your attention, most of all the attention of
the younger portion of my hearers, with no ordinary
authority. True economical science is sure to prove
of the greatest use to you throughout the whole
course of your lives; but you are entitled to ask,
' Is true science to be attained?' I desire to be quite
frank with you. It is not easy to obtain sound
economical science; on the contrary, it is most hard.
Not at all on account of the inherent difficulty of
the subject: if it were as difficult as mathematics or
electricity, its teaching would be far more precise, and
its results more certain. It suffers from the opposite
cause, from the ease with which every one talks of
Political Economy matters, and the fatal quickness
with which opinions are taken up about them. Above
all, the pursuit of Political Economy has to contend
against two peculiar and most formidable embarrassments. One of them assails it from within and the
other from without, and both combine to generate
a vagueness, an unsteadiness of utterance and belief,
which have little of the quality of true science. It is
a land of dispute and of controversy, of assertion and

denial. These features it possesses in common with many other sciences, with metaphysics for instance; but, unlike metaphysics, the conflicting opinions are not held firmly, clearly, and consistently. Hence it is grievous to confess, it is also a region in which little progress is definitively acquired and retained. There are few points accepted as established from which no one dares to differ, and still less which are used as starting-points for fresh developments. Whence spring these unwelcome occurrences? The science has been studied and professed by men of conspicuous ability, of wide-spread knowledge and of world-wide celebrity. The effect they have produced has been undoubtedly vast. They have revolutionized important departments of thought; they have set many powerful principles in motion over the world; they have told on the legislation of all civilized countries; and yet, somehow, we do not associate with Political Economy that feeling of accuracy, of settled knowledge, of truth won, and henceforth never to be contradicted, which constitutes our idea of a genuine science. I am constrained to acknowledge that Political Economy finds itself, even at this time of day, in a most unsatisfactory position. Two causes, it seems to me, have mainly brought about this result. The first and most influential is the singularly undefined character of the boundary line which incloses the subject-matter of Political Economy. The example set by the illustrious expounder of Political Economy has not been faithfully observed by his successors. In the 'Wealth of Nations,' the frontier line which separates Political Economy from cognate sciences is rarely transgressed. Adam Smith seldom runs away from his true subject, or mixes it up with foreign elements. His followers have too often written in a less philosophical spirit. Political Economy is infested with an incessant tendency to commingle with general politics. The confusion was natural : for wealth and finance form a large part of the business which occupies every Government; and a philosophy which augmented the riches of a people, stimulated their industry, poured expanding streams into the National Exchequer, and spread content-ment with prosperity over the country, could not fail to look exceedingly like the science of good government. And so it is in a sense : but still only within the limits of its appropriate province. But to identify Political Economy with statesmanship, with the science of government, to suppose that a great Political Economist is *ex vi termini* a great states-man, is as absurd as to identify the science of juris-prudence or of building iron-clads with politics, or to imagine that a great general is infallibly a scientific statesman. This confusion has shown itself in other branches of knowledge which are largely made use of by Governments ; but nowhere has it prevailed so widely or worked so much mischief as in Political Economy. Its name is unfortunate, and only too well calculated to precipitate its writers into this delusion. They never seem quite able to escape the impression that Political Economy is a branch of politics. It is a branch of politics in the same sense as the administration of war or of justice, and in no other. Politics is the master science, and Political Economy nothing more than a subordinate. It may be very important ; it may furnish more occupation to the statesman than any other province of human life ; it may have to be consulted more frequently,

and its suggestions may be very closely connected
with the happiness of the whole people; nevertheless
it is the knowledge of a single department only. Its
conclusions are not final, nor supreme. They may
be over-ridden, modified, or rejected at the dictation
of a yet more universal science, by the order of still
wider and higher knowledge. The function of the
economist is solely to report on the matters within
his cognisance to the statesman; but it is the statesman, and the statesman alone, whose prerogative it
is to judge of their application.

Instances of this distinction may readily be given.
It is conceivable, for instance, that under certain
circumstances of climate a particular race, such as
the negroes, might alone be capable of cultivating
the soil, and that such a race could be so employed
only under the condition of slavery. These are facts
which it would be the duty of the Political
Economist, on such a case arising, to report to the
politician. It would be entirely within his province
to point out that under such conditions the best
cultivation and the largest production of wealth
would be obtained. But there his function would
end. A moral consideration would then present
itself, whether such a mode of procuring riches ought
to be permitted. To estimate the weight due to this
element of the matter would be the statesman's office:
and obviously it would be his duty to give precedence
to the moral above the economical consideration. He
might not be able to deny the correctness of the
economist's reasoning; but he could not hesitate to
repel a conclusion which would be an offence against
a higher law than that which prescribed the accumu-
lation of wealth. Or, take again the law in France,

which enjoins the equal division of his land amongst
the children of a deceased father. As in the preceding example, it would be again the proper function
of the economist to estimate the effects of such a law
on the cultivation of the land and the productiveness
of agricultural industry in France. It might be his
office to submit to the legislator that such a law of
inheritance sentences France to small properties, to
their frequent sale and resale, to insufficiency of
capital for successful cultivation, to great difficulties
of drainage and manuring, and the like; and on
economical grounds, as an expert called in to com-
municate his professional knowledge, he would be
entitled to propose the substitution of the free liberty
of testation for the iron rule of equal division which
governs inheritance in France. But what answer
would he, as an economist, have for the Frenchman
who replied that the law of equal division amongst
children was implanted in the human heart by the
Creator, and that it was a thousand times better not
to offend against a moral feeling than to grow richer
by its violation? He would be silenced, and he
would have no ground for complaint; for his
authority does not extend over the whole of human
life. The teachings of his science have to be combined with the injunctions of other sciences; and it
is the political man alone, the statesman, who is
authorized to measure and compare the diverse re-
commendations of the several departments of knowledge. It rests with him to say what is the final
resultant which comes out from the combination of
all the considerations involved; and if the Frenchman's feeling about the law of nature to bequeath
property equally among children is to be refuted,

the refutation must be made by the philosophical politician.

It is easy to perceive that this unfortunate confusion breeds much harm to the study and the reputation of Political Economy. The quality of the science is injured by the admixture of foreign and often disturbing elements. Its writers are incessantly tempted to claim an authority in the political government of nations which is not warranted by their special attainments in one of its branches, and not unfrequently mounts up to arrogance. The facts of Political Economy, from their very nature, have, no doubt, a political side; for the industrial condition of the people must always be closely connected with their social and political life. It is natural that the scientific economist should be eager to carry out by law those improvements which his study of economical facts has revealed to him; and he will be the more impatient to accomplish this good work in proportion as he is a man of superior ability and lively sympathy. And if his action always followed this course,—if he analysed and deduced first, on the strictly economical ground, and then, stepping forth avowedly as a politician, urged upon statesmen the practical adoption of his conclusions,—no exception could be taken to his conduct, whilst the public weal would be promoted. His science would be respected, because it was science gathered and digested within its own legitimate province; and his success or failure in the political advocacy of his economical proposals would have no mischievous rebound on his scientific authority. But events seldom march along this wise and consistent path. It is far more common to find political feeling intruding

itself into the study of economical facts, impart-
ing to them a bias from without, colouring the
lessons which they teach and applying them to
political ends, to objects quite distinct from the
purposes of Political Economy; and what is the
inevitable effect of such a spectacle on the public
mind? The political feeling is plainly discerned,
even when the economist himself is unconscious of
its influence. It is inferred that Political Economy
is brought in to promote politics. The arrangements
of the facts, the emphasis given to their several
elements, the conclusions they are described as
yielding, are suspected; and the final result is the
feeling, which meets us on every side, of half respect
for, half distrust of, Political Economy. The public
does not bow down to the assertions of the economist
as it submits to the utterances of a physician or
a barrister. The true dignity of the science is
defaced.

Let us look for a moment at one of the most
keenly debated questions of our day, peasant-proprietorship. No subject is more deserving of attention and impartial examination. Peasant-proprietorship exhibits facts of first-rate importance—
untiring and uncalculating industry, watchfulness,
care, labour freely bestowed by love, thrift, and
other moral virtues of like excellence. On the other
side an equally striking picture is presented by
tenant-farming—capital amply supplied by landlord
and farmer, scientific agriculture, extensive works
of draining and manuring, numerous flocks and
herds, and other social and personal merits. These
are fitting facts for the study of the economist, and
for their impartial record, without side-glances to

c

political considerations; but how hard it is to meet
with such a digest of dispassionate observation, and
on that account recognized by the world as a body
of truths invested with authority. Who does not
lament to perceive the presence of the feeling that
peasant-proprietorship is found in democratic France
and tenant-farming in aristocratic England, and that
this feeling has told on the colouring given to the
statements of facts? Who does not regret to observe
that the merits and shortcomings of each system are
portrayed in an interest different from that of pure
science, and are made to serve as instruments for
propagating or supporting political opinion? A pure
science of politics is a most difficult attainment in
such a country as England, in which almost every
man takes a part in their practice, and is exposed to
strong disturbing forces of interest or passion; but it
is otherwise with Political Economy. Its truths are
the results of the investigation of general laws, and
its status is professional and subordinate; for these
very reasons it admits of dispassionate and scientific
study. Its reports should be placed on the same
level with the reports of legal and sanitary commissions: and the more rigorously they are restricted
to this character, the more accurate will be their
views and the higher their authority.

The mistiness which covers the boundary line of
Political Economy is, in the main, responsible for a
charge which has often been brought against it. It
is an irreligious science, we are often told: it takes
no thought about religion or morals: its mind is set
on the acquisition of riches; how to gain wealth, for
either man or state, is its only care. It looks only
at the gross result. Provided that production be

the largest possible, it heeds not at what cost of
moral and social degradation it has been accomplished. It ignores moral and social relations. It
treats men and women as producing machines. It
sanctions atrocious principles. It preaches universal
competition, and makes every man the enemy of his
fellow. Such have been the hard thoughts conceived
at times of Political Economy; and I will not say
that the manner in which economical discussion has
been conducted has not at times given some foundation for such remarks. At any rate the true reply
consists in proclaiming with the utmost energy and
plainest distinctness the subordinate character of
Political Economy. It is not supreme over man's
destinies on earth. It rules over material objects;
but man's existence is something infinitely greater
than material. To accumulate riches was not the
sole nor the chief end of the creation of man; and
this truth should never be absent from the mind
of every political economist who values the true
honour of his science. On the other hand, to up-
braid the investigation of the laws which govern
the production of wealth as irreligious is a simple
absurdity, unless it be irreligious to be anything
else than poor. It is a mere truism to say that the
material part of civilization has high importance for
man; but if it is a right thing to be industrious,
to till the ground and reap its fruits, it cannot but
be right also to search out the methods by which
this inevitable function may be most successfully
performed. Irreligion, when there is irreligion,
makes its appearance when an exclusive pre-emi-
nence is given to the acquisition of wealth, when
other considerations are omitted, when no regard is

paid to the diverse elements of human nature. The economist is entitled to investigate the most prolific principles of material production; but he is not authorized—quite the reverse—to hold them up as supreme. Take, for instance, the employment of young children in hard labour. It may be that a larger production will be thereby attained, but assuredly the State has a duty to interfere in the name of a higher science, and to protect the mental and spiritual qualities of the young. So again with national education. It may be true—I do not say that it is—that the loss of work caused by sending young labourers to school diminishes the sum-total of commodities produced; yet no economist who has any respect for the constitution of man's being will dream of opposing this loss to the public education of the young. That his science is not final will ever be the feeling of the really scientific economist.

This weakness in Political Economy can never be completely cured. It is impossible to exclude social considerations entirely from its researches. The moral and social circumstances which accompany any particular form of the mechanical production can never, and ought never to, be kept out of sight. There are means of generating wealth so destructive of human life, or of all that renders it worth possessing, as to deserve immediate reprobation at the hands of the inquirer into whose field of investigation they may chance to occur. Then, further, the social effects of industrial employments react on the efficiency of labour, and thus, on purely scientific grounds, call for examination. It is perfectly possible that certain trades might yield a balance of material profit in certain localities, and yet injure more than benefit a nation. Again, it is equally certain that political and social institutions may generate economical effects, and as such cannot bar out the inquiries of the economist. The debateable land between Political Economy and Political and Social Science must always exist; for it is nature's decree that it should not be susceptible of positive demarcation. It must remain the joint property of both philosophies. The best corrective for the evil is thoroughly to recognize its character; and to cultivate diligently a true philosophical spirit in dealing with its phenomena. The economist must strive not to render social aspects the governing principles of his investigation; and the politician and the socialist must labour to prevent their special ideas and aims from guiding researches into the working of industrial arrangements. Each is bound to keep his own end primarily in view: the economist to inquire into the production of wealth, checking afterwards his results by so much of an appeal to social considerations as is inevitable; the statesman to receive the economist's report with the respect due to the authority of a special science, and then to weigh the expediency of its suggestions by reference to higher principles, of which he is the legitimate expounder.

So much for the first of the two great difficulties which weigh on the pursuit of Political Economy—the one, namely, which is derived from its own nature, and the subject-matter which it explores. I come now to the second—the one which assails it from without, and which, as far as I am aware, Political Economy alone of all the sciences is compelled to endure. It never seems to make a final

and permanent lodgment of any of its truths in
the public mind. They float on a tide which often
carries the vessel backwards as fast as it progresses
forwards. The tendency to backslide seems to be
incessant and irresistible, not from any fault of its
own, or for want of ability and demonstrating power
in its teachers, but from the strength of the adverse
forces which every one of its conclusions is cease-
lessly obliged to encounter. A centrifugal force is
ever acting on some large section of society—sometimes even on a whole population—which makes it
forget all that it has learnt, and draws it back into
the darkness of ignorance. In other sciences a truth
once won is won for ever. No one challenges the
principle of gravity, or acts in defiance of its laws.
No one slides back into the belief that the sun
revolves round the earth. No one contradicts the
truths once established by the chemist or the hy-
draulist. The reason of this difference of fortune
does not consist in the certainty attached to the
subject-matter of the one and the inherent uncer-
tainty of the other. Some of the positions reached
by Political Economy attain the quality of demonstration : and yet they are denied or ignored as
readily as if they were the hypothesis of an empiric.
They are not argued against and refuted ; no second
trial is summoned to re-test their value. They are
simply passed over, and then the error they were
supposed to have dispelled resumes its possession of
the public mind just as if it were the infallible sug-
gestion of instinct. It seems like lost labour to
waste instruction on those who listen and are convinced, and then, under some indescribable impulse,
rebel against the light. And what is this impulse ?

How is a phenomenon, apparently so discreditable to the human understanding, to be explained? How comes Political Economy to have been born under so unlucky a star as to be doomed to teach and to persuade only to be repudiated? The explanation is to be found in the ceaseless action of selfishness, in the never-dying force of class and personal interests, in the steady and constant effort to promote private gains at the cost of the whole community. The foremost lessons of Political Economy are directed against narrow visions of private advantage, and they strive to show how the welfare of each man is most effectively achieved by securing the welfare of all. But it seems otherwise to the natural mind. The immediate gain lies before it, can be seen and handled, and the law which demands its sacrifice in order to arrive at a wider and more prolific result appears to contradict the senses, and to bring ruin and not benefit in its train.

The reverses which have befallen the central principle of Free Trade furnish a painful but striking illustration of this strange fatality. If Political Economy has demonstrated anything, it has demonstrated the truth of the principle of Free Trade. There are few who would venture to enter the lists against it openly. The utmost that would be alleged in the way of direct argument would be to express a doubt as to the expediency of its application under particular circumstances. Yet we have only to turn our eyes to Australia, a powerful and intelligent colony, and we meet with the wonderful sight of tariffs, as we are told, avowedly proposed against the interests of the community in order to increase the gains of the few. The leaning towards Protection displays itself openly. The movement of each class of traders, as it seeks to eliminate competition and to render its own products indispensable to the Australian public, is too strong to be resisted by those whose minds are capable of wider observation. The same phenomenon has been visible at times in Canada.

But it may be said that colonies do not contain their natural proportion of thoughtful students, and that the advocacy of Protection indicates an original deficiency of instruction rather than a relapse from truth to error. But what shall we say, then, of the United States of America, a nation as renowned for its intellectual gifts as for its greatness and its material power? What is the spectacle which America presents at this very hour? A system of Protectionist tariffs guards her vast frontier against the importation of foreign wares, a system which for severity has never been surpassed, except by absolute prohibition. What is become of Political Economy in America? It may be known to her literary men, it may be studied in her schools and universities, but as a power in the world, as a science authorized to enforce verities, as a teacher of statesmen how to develop most successfully the prosperity of the nation, it is a non-existing thing. It is trampled under foot and ignored; its voice is no more heeded than the rustling of the wind. But let my younger hearers mark it well : truth is never despised with impunity. It is a melancholy and painful sight ; but you will do well to gather up the instruction it conveys. Observe the fearful penalty with which America atones for contemptuously turning her back upon the light. Political

Economy is avenged by national calamities, which we deplore for America's sake, and also for our own; for they react on us. American lips have proclaimed how industry languishes, and whole trades have been swept away, and ruin has overwhelmed once noble industries, and national impoverishment has visited those who have refused to buy of others.

America furnishes a second example of this centrifugal force, which drives nations to renounce what they had been taught by Political Economy. The defence of an inconvertible currency may be said to have disappeared from English literature. No public writer of any weight for years past has committed himself to so hopeless a cause. On the continent of Europe inconvertible currencies still linger in some states, but they are not defended on the ground of principle; they are excused on the plea of an overwhelming necessity. The nations who adopt them are the objects of a certain pity, as the victims of a misfortune which vanquishes their judgment. If we cross the ocean, the scene is changed. The great American people not only adopted an inconvertible currency under the pressure of a severe war, but fondly cling to it in peace. So little are they ashamed of it, so indifferent are they to Political Economy, that when their own finance minister commenced lately the suppression of what science pronounced to be a great economical evil, Congress stepped forward to retain the inconvertible greenbacks, and to stay the scientific hand of its intelligent minister.

And now what is the moral to be drawn from these ever-recurring sins against light and knowledge? That Political Economy is in possession of no truth?

That the experience of life, and the surer intelligence
of a whole people, refutes the illusions with which
a few subtle thinkers bewilder themselves in the
closet? That practice is wiser than theory? Nothing
of the kind. Such practice contains no refutation
of theory; it puts forward no argument, it makes
no appeal to reason, it pretends to no better thought-
out opinions. We can trace here only the action of
disturbing influences, the power of selfishness in
combination with the most limited narrowness of
vision. The moral to be drawn is the importance
of thoroughly imbuing the mind with accurate principle before prejudice has had time to build itself
up, whilst the mind is impressible by reason, and
truths firmly implanted retain their hold for life.
The more you see nations and legislatures carried
away by the strength of the tide into narrow em-
piricisms, determine resolutely to be good Political
Economists. And do not imagine that there is less
need for accurate study in England than in more
youthful countries. We have just seen what back-
slidings men have been capable of abroad; let us
look now at what we say and do at home. The sight
will not encourage any sense of superiority that we
are better than others. Our country plumes herself
on her Political Economy. She gave birth to its
founder. No name is more revered amongst her
people than that of the great Scotchman who gave
to the world that masterpiece of common sense, the
'Wealth of Nations.' No book of these modern times
is encircled with a brighter halo of fame. There
is no authority with which a cultivated Englishman
would less like to be charged with being at variance
on a fundamental point, than Adam Smith. Well,

chief among the delusions which it was the aim
of the 'Wealth of Nations' to dispel, was the far-
famed mercantile theory. So thoroughly did Adam
Smith perform this task, so luminously did he
expose the absurdity, the irrationality, of the ruling
doctrines of the commercial world, that the mercantile theory has taken its place amongst the barbarous ideas of the ages of darkness. Since its
triumphant analysis, it stands side by side in public
estimation with such beliefs as that the earth is the
centre of the universe. Tell a great merchant or
banker of the City that he believes in the mercantile
theory, and he will resent the imputation as an
affront to his understanding. Now what is this
discredited mercantile theory? I cannot better describe it than in the words of Mr. Mill:—'It was
assumed in the whole policy of nations that wealth
consisted solely of money, or of the precious metals,
which, when not already in the state of money, are
capable of being directly converted into it. According to the doctrine then prevalent, whatever tended
to heap up money or bullion in a country added to
its wealth. Whatever sent the precious metals out
of a country impoverished it. If a country possessed
no gold or silver mines, the only industry by which
it could be enriched was foreign trade, being the only
one which could bring in money. Exportation of
goods was favoured and encouraged, because, the
exported goods being stipulated to be paid for in
money, it was hoped that the returns would be
actually made in gold and silver. The commerce
of the world was looked upon as a struggle among
nations which should draw to itself the largest share
of the gold and silver in existence; and in this com-

petition no nation could gain anything, except by
making others lose as much, or, at the least, prevent-
ing them from gaining it.' Mr. Mill then proceeds
to remark, ' It thus appears that the universal belief
of one age of mankind becomes to a subsequent age
so palpable an absurdity, that the only difficulty
then is to imagine how such a theory can ever have
appeared credible. It has so happened with the
doctrine that money is synonymous with wealth.
The conceit seems too preposterous to be thought
of as a serious opinion. It looks like one of the
crude fancies of childhood, instantly corrected by
a word from a grown person.'

Here, then, is the mercantile theory, and here is
what an eminent economist thinks of it, and his
opinion is re-echoed, in sound at least, by every other
person in the land. Now let us take up the newspapers of to-day. Read the City articles of every
one of them. Look at the cast of thought, at the
style of the literature, at the principles proceeded
upon, at the whole spirit of the language. What is
thought most deserving of record? The sums of gold
taken to the Bank of England, or taken away from
it: the amount of the bullion: the vessels laden
with gold on their passage to England from California and Australia: the state of the exchanges.
The beloved phrase of the mercantile theory, 'favourable exchanges,' is dwelt upon with satisfaction:
unfavourable exchanges and the departure of gold
to foreign countries are bemoaned with anxiety as
a loss: prognostications are made of a flourishing or
languishing trade, according to the influx or reflux of
the bullion: and weekly returns are proclaimed of
ingots buried out of sight in the cellars of the Bank.

The doctrine that gold is wealth—the doctrine which Mr. Mill paints as an absurdity so palpable that the present age regards it as incredible, as a crude fancy of childhood—breathes in every line of the City articles of all our daily newspapers. Traders are exhorted to carry on their operations with confidence, and to send their orders boldly to China and Japan, for gold is coming in, and discount is sure to be low. But if Englishmen are found to be buying food and clothing and raw materials from abroad, and are paying for them in gold, the merchants are warned to prepare for a coming storm: panic is at hand, and a crisis imminent, for the foreigner is getting hold of the staff of life, and England is losing it. It is not one paper or two which is saying all this, it is all. Every City article is penetrated through and through with the belief that the importation of gold is a good thing, and its exportation a bad one. The same thought, the same language pervades every counting-house, and is heard on every exchange. The unhappy man who should say aloud that he was glad to see gold leaving England would be gazed upon as a Rip van Winkle, who had re-appeared from the dead. What is this, I ask, but the mercantile theory, pure and fresh, as you heard Mr. Mill describe it? What is it but the resurrection of the Practical Man, the re-assertion of himself, of his experience, his appeal to outward form, to what may be touched and handled? The world fondly imagined that he was vanquished and gone; that Adam Smith had finally disposed of him: that boys and students had learnt to pity him, and to pride themselves on having been born after the great Scotch genius. Never was there a greater mistake.

It takes many Adam Smiths in Political Economy
to kill off for ever genuine mercantile superstitions.
The great authority, the man of millions, who
is supposed to understand the theory of business,
precisely because he has made millions, revives in
every age. ' Uno avulso, non deficit alter, Aureus.'
The mercantile theory may be consigned by philosophers to the limbo of nursery toys, but it lives on
all the same, and is master of the mind of the City,
and is supreme over City articles, and regulates the
barometer of commercial weather, and, above all,
is held to know the great secret of trade, and to be
able to show men the way to get rich.

The mercantile theory lives, and one of two inferences from this fact must be accepted. Either
it is the true theory of trade, and Adam Smith is
not the great benefactor of mankind which he is
supposed to have been ; or else, in the department
of science which has for its object the wealth of
the community, error possesses a vitality which is
more than a match for the keenest logic and the
strongest common sense.

The mercantile theory has given birth to a child
to which the whole literature of the world offers no
parallel, the doctrine of currency as exhibited in the
nineteenth century. I fear almost to utter its name,
—and yet it will form the subject of the following
lectures. The very sound of the word 'currency'
makes every man turn his back or shut his ears ;
his immediate instinct is to fly from a subject with
which he associates every kind of jargon and un-
endurable phraseology. Yet it was the very re-
pulsiveness of currency which induced me first to
embark upon its study. It seemed to me a marvellous

phenomenon, well worth investigation, that there
should be, at this period of the world's history, an
article of the most universal use in daily life, which
seemed to defy explanation in plain and intelligible
language. Other subjects of the most recondite
abstruseness had been mastered; hieroglyphics had
been read; mysterious inscriptions cleared up; the
profoundest depths of physics sounded, and the most
subtle problems in mathematics conquered. Few,
indeed, might be the hearers that these successful
investigators could attract; but those hearers listened
with delight, and could feel that they had made an
acquisition of real knowledge. What, then, was this
so-called science, from which all seemed to turn away
in disgust, even those whose lives were spent in
handling the objects of which it treats? How was
so astonishing an event to be explained? What
causes had rendered currency the reproach of our
age? What was there in sovereigns and banknotes
so inscrutable as to baffle the sharpest intellect, and
to be incapable of clear and simple exposition? The
cause of this strange spectacle presently became
evident. The philosophical spirit had been absent;
the right method of investigation had been, I will
not say neglected, but absolutely despised. The
method of Bacon, to which modern science owes its
strength, patient and accurate analysis, had been
scorned, as if fit only for physical subjects, but
too mechanical for such subtle substances as the
instruments of finance. *A priori* assumptions prevail
on every side in the discussion of currency. Every
one starts from some arbitrary hypothesis; can
one wonder after that to find universal confusion
and obscurity? Currency has become the jumble

that it is, authority contradicts authority, no first
principles are recognized as the common basis from
which reasoning may take its origin, and when some
practical measure has to be discussed, the cry of
salvation for commerce is met by the counter-shriek
of ruin, with an equal absence on both sides of an
admitted foundation for argument, simply because no
one will condescend to analyse facts, and to explore
their meaning. The world has chosen to defer to
great bankers and merchants, to men who have conducted vast businesses, and have realized gigantic
fortunes. These men, the world has said, have spent
their lives in dealing with money. Must they not
know the nature of money and its laws? Must we
not take our theory at their hands? And so mankind did take the theory of money from commercial
authorities, and the result has been currency in the
state in which we now find it.

A right method of investigation will easily give
currency its legitimate place amongst clear and intelligible sciences. We have only to keep currency
rigorously separate from matters with which it is
associated in practice, but has no community of
nature whatever, and then to examine its own natural
phenomena, and we shall be surprised to discover
what a simple thing it will prove itself to be. I have
no fine-spun theory to lay before you; no subtle
creed about money raised on a foundation of assumption, and sustaining itself with phraseology utterly
dark for the common understanding. The exposition
I propose to submit to you is something far more
commonplace and unpretending. The result I
arrive at is simply the demonstration that currency obeys the ordinary laws which belong to all

commodities. No one experiences any difficulty in understanding the action of these laws on the other material substances which civilization employs. I hope to convince you that the recognition of these laws is capable of dispelling all obscurity from currency.

LECTURE II.

METALLIC CURRENCY.

BEFORE commencing the investigation of Currency I have two requests to make of you, which I desire to press with all possible emphasis. I pray you, in the first place, to come to the examination of the analysis which I shall lay before you with minds free from all pre-conceived opinion. If such a request seems to require an apology from me, I freely offer it: but I beg you to remember that the main cause of the confusion which besets currency is the fatal ease with which a few apparently obvious, but hasty and incoherent, ideas take possession of the understanding and indispose it to all patient and accurate investigation. As long as the mind remains in this state there is no good to be done; the present Babel must continue, and the name of Currency must remain as repulsive as ever. True science alone is clear and consistent, and there is only one road to true science, only one foundation on which it can rest, a thorough analysis of the facts, and a firm determination to accept what they teach

D 2

and nothing else. The surest way to get rid of arbitrary and *à priori* hypothesis is to begin from the beginning; and in no other field of thought is this method of going to work more imperatively called for than in currency. On the other hand, I must beg you to deal with what I shall say with the utmost severity. Challenge my investigation with unsparing rigour: and above all watch with the utmost care that I make no omissions. In dealing with ultimate facts and the construction of first principles, not to perceive, and consequently not to give, its due weight to any element of a subject is as disastrous as to misconceive and misapprehend. An omitted truth, an unobserved elementary fact, ruins the scientific edifice. The rest of the foundation may be solid, but an unexplored spot may bring the whole building to the ground. To observe accurately, but also to observe fully, is the one sound basis of all science.

My second request flows immediately from my first. Having analysed with care, be true to the principles you have gained. Bring your logic to bear unflinchingly on subsequent explorations: especially be not afraid of it. It is no true science if it cannot bear the application of logic in drawing inferences. When therefore you have gained first principles from analysis, apply them rigorously to every detail: and when a difficulty occurs, of which at the time you are not able to see the explanation, take the greatest care not to be faithless to the principles you have won. This danger exhibits itself in a peculiarly insidious form in currency. I have rarely found men of any intelligence contest the first principles yielded by analysis. They are, on the contrary, almost uni-

versally accepted as truths so obvious as hardly
to require statement. But the next moment those
who were so impatient to assent come out with
views in direct variance with the principles they so
readily acknowledged; and then, when pressed with
the contradiction, they pour out floods of arbitrary
doctrine, which they do not pretend to have gained
from analysis, and are almost sure to end with
abusing their fellow-converser as a theorist. Let
us adopt a wiser method. Let us acquire our first
truths with a sound intellectual conscience: and that
done, let us judge every subsequent problem fearlessly
by a rigorous application of these first truths. We
may not always be able at the time to trace out the
point at which elaborate and perplexing systems
of error have diverged from the right path; but
we can, and we ought always to be able to, say
firmly that they are wrong, because their conclusions
contradict first principles. No doubt, this is a high
intellectual faith; but every scientific man possesses
it in his own region: why should it not be found
in currency also?

I now proceed to the consideration of the nature
and functions of currency. I shall speak first of
metallic currency, or coin, not only because it is the
most ancient, the most general, and the most easily
understood form of currency, but also because it
furnishes peculiar facilities, from its simplicity, for
ascertaining the fundamental laws of all currency.
A coin is a very intelligible matter compared with
a bill or a banknote: and it is an enormous advantage at the origin to lay aside the complications
which encumber the paper instruments of exchange.
It is in these paper substitutions for metal that

dogmatic assertion, with its attendant confusion, loves
to lurk. A large part of the language which meets
our ears upon currency would be impossible, if the
utterers were strictly confined to coin: and as
coin in all countries plays, if not the largest, yet
certainly the most important, part in effecting exchanges of property, in buying and selling, it is
plain that a thorough understanding of the operation
of coin involves substantially all the great principles
of currency.

Currency has its origin in the division of labour.
No man can supply all his own wants himself: no
one can knead his own bread, make his own coat,
and build his own house at the same time. No man
can avoid calling in the assistance of his neighbours
in procuring these things, and they in turn are
equally obliged to have recourse to his aid. It was
soon perceived that the man who confined his labour
to the manufacture of one single article acquired
a skill which enabled him to produce much more
in the same time and much better: and in this way
the progress of civilization led to the distribution of
employments amongst men, each severally creating
a commodity which all consumed. The articles
having been produced, the next step was to exchange them: how was this to be done? Direct
barter, direct exchange of one article against the
other, was the first method employed: it was the
most ancient, but it exists to this hour also. In
every country a certain number of exchanges of
one thing for another continually occur. But direct
barter was exposed to a difficulty, which, if not
removed, would have been fatal to the growth of
civilization. The tailor who was hungry might not

be able to find a baker who wanted a coat. The coatless mason might search in vain for a tailor who desired to build. A great nation could not have grown up with no other means of exchanging but barter. But this was not the only perplexity: a second, equally embarrassing, made its appearance at the same moment. How was the comparative worth of the two commodities to be exchanged to be ascertained? How was the tailor to discover how many loaves he ought to get for his coat, or the mason to learn how much brickwork he was to make for the garment? These were two very formidable embarrassments for the necessary business of exchanging, of buying and selling; some way of overcoming them had to be discovered, or a civilized society could not have existed. A very natural and very effective remedy was found, so natural as to have sprung up of itself, for I believe there is no record of its having been originally the creation of law. Men agreed by common consent to select some single commodity, which all should be willing to take in exchange for the products of their labour. Each gave his goods for this intermediate article, because he knew that every other producer would be ready to do the same. The tailor was instantly relieved from the danger of starving, the mason had no longer any anxiety about procuring clothing. This medium of exchange, as it is sometimes called, removed the difficulty. The baker, the tailor, and the mason were certain to be able to obtain with it the articles which they severally needed. It also solved the second perplexity. It supplied the indispensable convenience of a measure of value: it provided the means of learning the comparative worth of every

commodity. This comparative worth is measured
by identically the same process as that by which
the length or weight of anything is ascertained.
When we desire to learn how long an object is, we
place it side by side with a rod, arbitrarily chosen,
which we call a yard, or metre, or the like; and
then we say that the object is so many yards long.
So again with weight: we compare the body whose
weight we seek to know with the gravity of a lump
of iron, of known size, or of a volume of water,
which we call a pound or by some other name; and
when we say that a thing has such or such a weight,
we mean that its gravity equals that of so many of
these pieces of iron or volumes of water. Precisely
in the same way men choose an intermediate commodity which they interpose between what they
have to sell and what they seek to buy; and value
means the quantity of this interposed commodity
for which every other article can be exchanged.

Very many substances have been used in different
ages and amongst different nations as this medium
of exchange, but metals have generally been preferred. Of these, copper, silver, and gold have been
most extensively employed. It is sufficient to mention in this place, that the precious metals, as they
are called, gold and silver, have ultimately been
chosen by civilized nations as the most fitting materials for making coin. They are clean to handle,
beautiful to look on, hard and durable, capable
of being divided into small pieces, of high intrinsic
value, and consequently very portable; and above
all, especially gold, as little subject to changes of
actual intrinsic worth as any other material which
could be used as an universal instrument of ex-

change. These are the reasons which have led to the selection of gold and silver for the purposes of currency. Small portions of these metals, of definite purity and weight, are manufactured into coins by the State, and a national stamp put upon them, to authenticate this purity and weight. In England these coins are called shillings, crowns, sovereigns, and so on. Their true nature then is easy to be understood. They are simply bits of metal, whose weight and purity are attested by the stamp of the State : they are absolutely nothing more. The stamp tells every man who consents to take a sovereign for his goods that it contains nearly a quarter of an ounce of pure gold : and then the seller, knowing this fact, settles for himself how many of these sovereigns he will ask for his wares. And thus we learn what a pound is, a question of absurd celebrity, but one which is very mischievously misunderstood by many writers on currency. The word 'pound' is the legal name for a sovereign ; and its simple meaning is, that when men speak of pounds in bargains and contracts, the law will interpret the expression to mean a sovereign, a coin containing so much gold of known fineness. By stamping them, the State supplies all buyers and sellers with a piece of knowledge indispensable for all sales, the knowledge, namely, of the quality and quantity of the metal of the coin for which goods are given away. The State reserves to itself, and rightly reserves, the monopoly of minting or coining—not for the reason no longer tenable in modern political philosophy, that coining is a personal prerogative of royalty, but because the State is undeniably the best stamper that can be procured, the person who can give the surest guarantee to the

public that the coin, the sovereign, does really contain
the weight and purity which it professes to have.
And if the State can do the work best, the public
interest demands that it should alone be authorized
to perform it. If there were no national Mint, the
want of the public to know what a piece of gold
offered on a purchase really was would lead to eminent merchants or bankers affixing their own brands
to their own pieces of gold. The result would be
that Baring's money, Rothschild's money, and all sorts
of money would be circulating together, and the
confusion would be intolerable. The authentication
of no private person can give a warranty as trustworthy as that of the State.

These pieces of metal, these coins, are called money,
and we are now able to understand their nature and
their functions. The tailor is willing to sell for
money. No law obliges him to do so. He may ask
a sheep for his coat if he pleases : he sells for money
of his own free will, because he knows that every
other tradesman will do the same. This knowledge
gives him a perfect guarantee, that by adopting the
intermediate process of selling for money, he will be
certain to attain his real object, namely, the acquisition of other articles which he wants, and which
he thus procures in exchange for his coat. He is
no longer under the necessity of hunting out a baker
who is in want of a coat : he sells the coat for money,
and with that money he buys bread, for the baker,
though in no need of a coat, wishes to build, and he
knows he can set the mason to work with the money
he got from the tailor. Through the agency of the
money, the coat is exchanged for its equivalent
value of other commodities, the tailor, by accepting

money, having acquired the power of choosing those commodities according to his wants and inclinations.

The value of any commodity is the quantity of metal—in England, omitting silver, the quantity of gold—for which it can be exchanged; and this quantity of metal is called its price. The price of an estate, of a horse, of a house, is the number of sovereigns, that is, the weight of metal, which can be obtained for it. This is a very simple statement, but it is also one which you cannot remember too carefully. It is one about which endless misapprehension prevails: and as no word is so important in currency as 'value,' you will do well to recollect always that value means the weight or quantity of gold which anything will fetch.

I have dwelt in full detail on this analysis because our tailor, baker, and mason are complete representatives of the whole commercial world. It is very easy to be mystified by the magnitude and complications of modern trade, and to think that they involve some mysterious and indescribable influences; but this is a pure illusion. The vast operations of commerce, when dissected, only reproduce the action of the tailor and his two fellow-tradesmen. Their wares are faithful images of the goods in shops and warehouses: the scissors and the trowel are as real machines as the grandest steam-engine: mills, however vast, are only expanded tailors' rooms: foreign trade, with its ships on every sea, is only the baker's boy carrying the loaves round; and the City is fully found in the tailor's accounts of money due by him for wool, and money owed to him by customers. We must not be misled by mere mag-

nitude ; and since the occurrences described contain
all the essential elements of all trade, we may apply
ourselves with entire confidence to extracting from
them the principles they yield.

1. In the first place, it is evident that money is
not sought by any one for its own sake. It is a
means to an end, but not the end itself. It is a tool,
an instrument, procured solely for the sake of the
work it performs ; just as a spade or a mill is bought
solely out of regard to the potatoes or the yarn
which it will enable its owner to produce. Many
people speak as if money was a thing good and
desirable for its own sake. The wish to have money
seems to be a complete thing in itself : the remainder
of the thought, that money has to be got rid of, is
in constant abeyance. Money is worthless unless it
is used ; and it is not used till it is parted with.
I omit for the present the consideration of stocks
of money required by bankers and others, just as a
grocer keeps a stock of tea, or a wine-merchant of
wine. Money is an article as much on sale as a hat
in a shop. A sovereign is no better than a pebble,
or a jewel, if you will, until it is employed in buying
something. The tailor does not buy money with
his coat because he wishes to wear the sovereigns
as ornaments. He can neither feed nor clothe himself with sovereigns, but only with the food and
wool which the sovereigns on leaving him place in
his hands. Money is nothing but an interposed
commodity, the very end of whose existence is to
be got rid of with all practicable speed. When,
therefore, bankers tell the world that it is of the
utmost importance to trade to keep gigantic treasures of money in a cellar, they impose upon them-

selves the burden of proving that they know what money is, that they understand its object and function, and that large masses of money which are never touched, and within all human probability never will be touched, are not a practical and scientific absurdity.

2. In the next place, we perceive that the use of money substitutes double for single barter. It involves two distinct acts for reaching the end desired; and each of these acts is an act of barter. The object of the tailor is to get bread; and he obtains the bread by first bartering his coat for money, and then bartering back the money for bread. The obtaining of bread is his motive for making and selling the coat; and the money through which he arrives at the bread is as much machinery as his scissors. Every sale for money is only half a transaction. The transaction is not completed till the money has bought other articles. Money is always seeking to buy; money hoarded or not used is for the time annihilated as money. It is a field left uncultivated; it ceases to be a portion of the nation's capital.

3. Thirdly, since a sale for money is an act of barter, it follows that the conditions are the same on both sides of the bargain. Common usage applies the word 'selling' to the man who has the commodity, and the word 'buying' to him who has the money; but the expressions 'buying' and 'selling' apply equally to both. No difference whatever exists in the position of the two men who engage in a sale. All the circumstances incident generally to commodities belong to the thing sold and to the money alike. Coats, bread, fish, and all other things, may

be produced in excess beyond the wants of the day, and are not saleable, except at a reduction of price. It is exactly the same with gold or money, however paradoxical it may sound. Sovereigns in circulation become unsaleable at certain periods of the year, and flow back to the bank, rather than submit to a diminution of value. Gold can easily be produced in excess, beyond the use and demand for it; and it not only can, but has been actually so produced. And what has been the consequence?—that gold has had to endure the fate of all commodities in excess; it has sunk in value; its producers, the miners, have had to take fewer commodities in exchange for it, before they could get people to buy it. And thus it has happened that gold is worth some fourteen times less than in the days of the Henrys. Compared with the demand for it, a great deal too much was produced; but the miners, though getting much less for each single ounce of the metal, went on working, because they found they could extract gold from the mine with corresponding cheapness of cost. In this way the excess disappeared: two sovereigns were produced for one; but two at ten shillings each were required to do the same work as one at twenty, for the intrinsic worth of the two depreciated sovereigns only equalled that of the original one.

4. This equality of position in both buyer and seller leads up to a very important question—What is the value of gold? The words 'value' and 'price,' as we have seen, when used of other commodities, mean the quantity of gold which they can be exchanged for; but how shall we, on the other side, express the value of gold? Put in this form, the

question admits of no single answer. The price and
value of the sovereign is a hat for the hatter, so
many loaves for the baker, so many pounds' weight
of wool for the farmer, and so on throughout the
whole list of things sold. A hat is the price of the
gold, just as a sovereign is the price of the hat.
But the answer we are in search of will be found
in the analysis of what is implied in an act of barter.
What is the value of the coat to the tailor? Before
he sells, how has he calculated the worth of his coat,
and so formed a notion of the quantity of bread or
other commodity which he ought to obtain in exchange
for it? Clearly he calculates what the work cost
him, how much he gave for the wool, how much
labour he spent on the job, how much food and
clothing he consumed whilst employed upon it, what
rent he had to pay, and so on. In other words, he
estimates the worth of the coat by its cost of production. The owner of the gold does identically the
same thing, either he or the miner who got it out of
the mine. A certain amount of tools, materials, and
labour was expended in obtaining the gold just as in
manufacturing the coat; and when those quantities
are held to be equal by both the parties, the bargain
is struck, and the sale is effected. If the miner fails
to obtain for his gold a quantity of goods sufficient
to replace what he has consumed in mining, with
a reasonable profit for himself, he gives up the business, and abandons the mine. Less gold is then
produced, and, if the demand for it remains the same,
it rises in value; it exchanges for a larger quantity
of other articles, and a smaller piece of the metal will
buy the same amount of commodities in the shops.
In other words, the prices of all commodities fall.

If, on the contrary, the mining has yielded larger supplies of gold for the same labour and capital, precisely as a good harvest increases the number of ricks in the farm-yard, the miner can afford to take fewer commodities for his gold. Gold then exchanges for less—a larger piece of metal is required to buy the same quantity of goods—that is, all prices rise. Thus a rise in general prices marks that gold has become cheaper, and a fall that it has become scarcer and dearer.

5. I now come to a question of supreme importance for a clear understanding of currency. It merits your closest attention ; for your power of dealing with theories on currency and with the language which you will hear on every side will be vastly increased, if you have thoroughly grasped this question and its answer. How much gold, how many sovereigns does a country want ? At first this question seems absurd. How can any one have too much money ? With money one can buy anything ; money then is true riches, and the more gold a nation can get the better. So says the mercantile theory, and so say the newspapers every day. They hail with delight every arrival of gold from Australia. But those who talk in this manner totally forget that gold has to be paid for like everything else. It is a very expensive affair to obtain gold out of a mine : a great deal of timber and tools and gunpowder and wages is consumed in the business, and the country which gets the gold has to pay for all these things. I have shown you already that it is possible for gold to be in excess. The true question then is, not the absurdity how much gold a country can take if given for nothing, but how much gold

does a country require so as to make it worth its while to buy it and pay for it with other commodities? The answer depends on the further question, How much gold can a nation use? How much can it find employment for? Let us see whether our analysis of the use of money, and our old acquaintances, the baker and the tailor, can help us to answer these questions.

It is obvious at once that if all three, the baker, the tailor, and the mason, sell their products at the same instant of time, in order to effect the barters there must be as large a value of gold as of all the other commodities bartered. Barter is an exchange of equivalents; and, as I have shown, every sale for money is an act of barter. But in the actual working of human life, the three sales do not take place simultaneously: the tailor does not sell his coat, the baker his bread, the mason his bricks, at the same moment. The sales take place at different times; and consequently the same sovereigns may effect all the three sales. Our three tradesmen are types of the whole world—all buyers and sellers do what they do. The quantity, therefore, of gold for which a nation ·can find use, and which consequently is wanted, depends on the number and amount of those sales in which gold is employed, and on the rapidity with which the same sovereigns, in the actual circumstances of the country, perform many sales or pay many debts. In a nation in which life moves slowly, or buyers and sellers dwell far asunder, or no credit is given and all purchases are for ready money, much gold, many sovereigns will be wanted in comparison with the quantity of buying and selling that goes on. On the contrary, in a town full of shops closely packed together, in which the movement of trade is rapid, and credit is largely given, and banks with clearing-houses exist in great numbers, few sovereigns are required, and those few circulate swiftly, and carry out many sales on the same day, and are needed in wonderfully smaller numbers in proportion to the work which they have to do. But in both cases alike, the tailor and the baker teach us the same lesson, that the quantity of coin needed by any country is what is actually wanted for buying the coat and the bread with money. The gold, therefore, which a nation wants and can use, is that amount only which is actually employed, which passes from hand to hand, which is reckoned on the counter, and which is carried about in men's pockets, including, of course, a certain reserve stock kept by gentlemen in their purses and tradesmen and bankers in their tills. There is no fixed rule, therefore, for every country alike. Many circumstances cause the quantity of coin used to vary extremely in different lands with the same identical amount of goods bought and sold; and we thus obtain a deduction of considerable scientific value, that the question of the distribution of the precious metals, on which so much stress is so often laid, is at bottom a question of the commercial habits of different countries. A nation is not the poorer for possessing little gold, nor the richer for having much: and I earnestly beg you to keep this truth in mind. The precious metals flow to countries of low civilization, of great political insecurity, which hoard money, and trade for cash; whilst they find small resting-place in lands of high commercial development, where property is safe and the recovery of debts easy, and the owners of goods are willing to part with them for cheques and bills and other processes of deferred payment. There is, probably, no country in the world which, in comparison of the extent of its business, wants and uses so little of the precious metals as England.

You will now ask, How is one to find out how much buying and selling and paying of debts with coin goes on in England, so as to discover how many sovereigns are needed? I reply, by putting to you a counter-question. How does a hatter or any other trader find out how many heads there are which require hats? He learns this by experiment. He makes a certain number of hats; if they go off, he makes more; if they remain on hand, he stops his manufacture. It is precisely the same with gold: it comes to England, and as much is taken into use as the country requires. If more arrives from Australia it cannot be used; it passes for a while into the chests of dealers in bullion or the vaults of the Bank of England. What happens then? you will ask again. What is the event with gold which corresponds with the hatter ceasing to make hats? It gradually takes flight abroad. The bullion-dealers export it to countries which require and can use it, to nations whose circumstances enable them to find room for more gold. Thus France and America took up most of the additional supplies from California and Australia, for substituting a gold in the place of their silver coinage: and the constant increase all over the world of trading and industrial establishments, which employ gold in paying salaries and wages, in travelling, in filling military chests, and the like, creates an ever-expanding demand for the metal.

But if the world were to be full and the miners went on increasing the supply beyond the demand, one of two things would inevitably happen : gold would become cheaper, as every other article does of which the supply exceeds the demand, or the miner, if he could not sell his gold cheaper, would do exactly what the latter did, he would cease to mine.

And here I must call your notice to a peculiar feature which distinguishes the cheapening of gold and coin from the cheapening of any other commodity. If meat or tea falls in price, the public is clearly benefited. Those who already have as much tea as they want, have less to pay for it, and those whose means prevented them from having their fill of tea are now able to buy more. The world is so much the richer. The world has a capacity for consuming more meat and tea, and the increased quantity produced, which caused the fall of the prices, is a positive increase of wealth. It is otherwise with gold and money. Cheaper gold to act as money is no gain ; nay, it is a real inconvenience, and might become a serious evil. The world does not want sovereigns to be as cheap as shillings, and shillings to be worth no more than pence. Every one would have to carry about twenty sovereigns where he now carries one : it would be an increase of weight, and nothing more. The distinction between coin and every other commodity consists in this,—that specific portions or pieces of other things are wanted, whilst of gold it is specific values. A definite piece of iron of given size is wanted for the rod of a suspension bridge ; if iron were cheapened, the rod would not be made larger, though two bridges might be made instead of one. But our analysis has taught us that the tailor and the baker called the gold in to furnish not a piece of given size or weight, but an equivalent of value. When the tailor barters his coat for gold, the barter is of equal cost of production on both sides. If the gold becomes cheaper, and its cost of production less, a larger quantity must be used in order to reach the same value. It is a matter of indifference to the tailor whether he gets one single sovereign, which costs twenty shillings to make, or eight sovereigns which cost half-a-crown each. In every case he must get the same cost of gold: a cheapening of gold, therefore, only leads to a larger weight of it being used for the same work: let it be ever so cheap, the number of sovereigns must always be made up to the coat's worth. After that, no more is wanted. If wool and scissors become cheaper, he may make more coats, and gain more profit, because more buyers may come in ; but the cheapening of coin can only burden him with more weight to carry. The public, then, in respect of currency, has no interest in buying gold more cheaply ; for weight is a most serious element in coin. You can imagine the perplexity and the annoyance if a sovereign were to become of no more value than a shilling. Every article in every shop would stand at a price twenty times higher: and those who remember travelling in France in the days of silver will know what the inconvenience is of carrying heavy sacks full of coin. Heavy coin is a nuisance of immense magnitude for a busy nation.

Our analysis, then, has taught us the fundamental principle that coin or gold is needed only for those particular purchases and payments which are actually

made by passing gold from one man's hand to another's; and that when there is enough for this
specific purpose any surplus must lie idle, and
can be redeemed from being a waste only by being
exported abroad, or by diminishing in value. It
is a great matter in currency to understand the
meaning of this word 'enough.' There are hats
enough when every head is covered; there is gold
enough when every man who wants change can
get it. Of course, more hats are actually in existence
than there are heads, else perchance some one might
suddenly find himself hatless: and so more gold
ought to be found in a country than is wanted for
change on any given day. But this is only an
incident which coin is subject to, like any other
kind of goods. I use this word 'change' designedly,
because I want to impress upon you with all the
emphasis in my power, that it is only for small
payments, for the small retail business of the country,
and what may be called 'change,' that gold is wanted
and used in England. I wish the feeling to come
to you naturally and spontaneously at all times,
when you hear gold spoken of, that this talk is
really only about the coin required for these very
minor payments. I think I have said enough to
show you how gigantic is the waste created by the
vast treasures of bullion buried in the great banks
of England and France; and we are able now to
tell the City and the newspapers that the exportation
of coin and unfavourable exchanges are often the
very things to be desired and to rejoice over. The
mercantile theory is destroyed by our analysis, or
our analysis is false.

6. What precedes will enable us to deal with views

and language which are repeated on every side.
We are told that the state of the circulation, that
is, the amount of the currency, the number of
sovereigns and banknotes moving about the country,
produces enormous effects on trade, on the resources available for merchants, on the business
of the City, and on the rates of interest which borrowers have to pay for loans. The law actually
compels the Bank of England to publish every week
reports of the quantity of gold which it possesses
and of the number of notes in circulation. Our
analysis furnishes no support for such opinions ;
nay, it is absolutely destructive of them. England,
we have seen, has a use for a certain number of
sovereigns and no more. There is a certain work
to be done by them, in making particular payments
with ready money, for travelling, and the like : and
the only interest she has in the quantity of the
circulation is that there should be sovereigns enough
to do this work. The quantity of the work, and
the number of sovereigns needed to perform it, is
a mere matter of statistics of the habits of the
population, but has no other importance than the
number of hats or umbrellas used in the country.
Merchants, and all except small tradesmen, do not
trade with sovereigns ; they do not borrow sovereigns, nor use sovereigns, except for small change.
A large arrival of sovereigns to-day from Australia
would not make merchants a whit more than any
person in this room use a single sovereign the more.
A few days ago, the City article of the 'Times' told
the world that much gold was coming into England,
and that it would seek investments here. This view
involves a fundamental error in Political Economy ;

it forgets that this gold cannot be invested in England, because England already has more than enough for the use it can be put to. It cannot be used; it must go into the lumber-room; it can be invested only by sending it abroad to countries who have a specific use for it. If the importers of this gold bought investments with it, the sellers of these investments would despatch it to the bank's cellars before the day was out. Why is there at this moment such a colossal sum of gold in the Bank of France at Paris? Because the trade of France is in that state that there is a diminished number of payments made with metal, and there being less work for the 'napoleons' to do, the unused ones flow back into the vaults.

A country can keep more gold in circulation on two conditions only. Either the number of payments made with gold (which in England are always only a very insignificant part of the total payments made in actual life) must increase, or else the intrinsic worth of the gold itself must be diminished, and then, as already shown, more sovereigns will be required to make the same payment, to effect the same act of barter and exchange. But in this latter case, the fall in the intrinsic value of the metal must be universal all over the world; for an Englishman, owning gold in England, will not let it go for less than twenty shillings in the pound, if he can obtain the same number of shillings in another country. The unused gold in London and Paris, now amounting to so vast a sum, is gold which its owners will not part with at a reduced value. It is gold waiting for use or for exportation to places where it is wanted. If it should be wanted nowhere, the fact would indicate that the stock of gold was become excessive at its actual worth all over the world, and a fall in its value would be at hand.

Such are the fundamental principles established by the examination of a purely metallic currency. It now becomes necessary to study the phenomena which money is made to exhibit, like every other article of consumption, in so complex an organization as a civilized nation. Foremost amongst these are the fluctuations which the use and demand for coin undergo. Few things are more variable than sales and purchases: there is not a single commodity which is not sold in different quantities, at different prices, at different times. The quantity of coin required for buying and paying must clearly correspond to the number and value of the sales effected directly by the agency of coin. More gold is required at one time than at another in England, as everywhere else. The habits of a people exercise considerable influence in this matter. The disposition to pay with ready money is not the same at all times. At this moment the spread of co-operative associations, which refuse credit and exact payments in cash, might largely increase the use and demand for sovereigns. On a yet larger scale, events affecting the whole nation constantly create fluctuations of far greater magnitude. A deficient harvest in England always necessitates large purchases of corn from foreign countries; and these in the first instance are payed for by an exportation of gold. It is the fashion to speak of such an event as a 'drain,' a word of unpleasant and ominous sound to the commercial imagination. Worse yet: war sometimes makes large demands for gold; and a call of this kind led to the suspension of its notes in cash by the Bank of England in 1797. How do these fluctuations act on a purely metallic currency? They occurred before the invention of paper money : they are incidents inherent in human life at all times. How were they met in the past? How are they dealt with now in those countries whose state of civilization does not admit of credit, or banks, and their numerous paper offspring? A country threatened with starvation must and will buy food abroad, if it has any property which foreigners will take in exchange for their corn ;—how does it manage the operation, especially when the quantity of gold it possesses is insufficient to purchase the corn that is needed? In order to answer these questions correctly, we ought to understand the process by which a nation buys merchandise of any kind from foreigners. It buys always with its own productions : it has nothing else to give ; and it cannot get without giving in return. England purchases corn and cotton from America, and pays for them with iron-ware, yarn, books, and other goods made in her own factories. Exact equivalents must be exchanged. Foreign trade is merely an aggregate of individual bargains, in which buyer and seller stipulate for equality on both sides. All foreign trade, therefore, must and does balance itself. Each nation sells as much as it buys. But there is a special difficulty in all foreign trade : the purchases balance—but not always on the same day, nor even for a considerable period of time. England may buy much more corn of America in a particular month than America buys of English iron. How is the balance to be maintained? How is the payment made? In the precise way in which the tailor

managed to sell his coat, though it was bread that
he wanted, and the baker was in no want of a coat:
America takes the difference in gold, though she
is in no want of gold for its own sake. She knows
that with this gold she can procure from other
nations goods that she really needs. Foreign trade,
thus, is an exchange of products between two nations, the products being in the long-run equal on each
side, and any deficiency which may occur on either
side for the time having to be made up with gold.
Let us now come back to the case supposed—a very
deficient harvest, and large and immediate purchases
of corn in America. The foreign trade with America
is at once thrown out of equilibrium. England buys
profusely, long before America buys of England in
return. A balance of gold must, it is obvious, pass
from England to America, and an exportation of
gold, with its unfavourable exchanges, is the most
excellent and salutary of remedies. However, the
quantity is not so large as might be expected: the
machinery of modern trade supplies a buffer which
lessens the pressure. Foreign commerce is not a
ready-money business; buyers do not pay cash down;
they are allowed to defer payment by signing bills
or obligations to pay at some later period. In this
way England buys the urgently-needed corn with bills,
at perhaps some three or six months' date; and by
the time that they are due, the Americans have
begun to buy in return with the money which they
know will presently be paid them, and the equilibrium
has commenced to be restored, before any large
quantity of gold has left England for America.
Some gold, however, does leave at once: how is
it procured when the currency is purely metallic?

Plainly from the stock in the hands of the English public. The task of finding it falls on those who send out orders for corn. They collect it, as they can, from the bullion-dealers, from their debtors, from those who have some gold, and are willing to send it to them. I purposely omit here to speak of the action of banks in this matter; for a bank is a very complicated institution, and it will be better to examine the operations of banks as a whole in a subsequent lecture.

Some gold is despatched at once to America in the case supposed. If England has enough to spare, no inconvenience is felt by any one: but it may be that the quantity available is insufficient. If that is so, and gold still goes out—for the necessity of procuring food is urgent—a deficiency must arise in England. Change runs short; the quantity of coin required for buying and selling is below what is needed; inconvenience is inevitable: what then, I ask, would happen? I hope you will allow me to repeat here what I have said elsewhere. ' What must one expect to see when an outflow of gold is established for a protracted period?' Writers on currency treat this as a special and terrible calamity, to be averted by every expedient, as a wound calling for amputation or any other desperate remedy: for my part, I can consider it only as an every-day occurrence of trade. Why, I ask myself, must a deficiency of gold be regarded as an event more alarming or more disastrous than a short harvest, or a scanty supply of cotton, or a scarcity of silk? Nay, I think rather, that of all deficiencies, there is none, for England at least, so easy and so sure to be supplied as a deficiency of gold. A famine of cotton we have learnt

to our cost may be very possible; equally so a
dearth of corn; but a famine of gold is next to
impossible, amidst the resources of a country like
England. Gold can be purchased all over Europe.
It requires no long loading in ships, or tedious delays
in docks. A letter or two from England would
fetch in twenty-four or forty-eight hours any quantity that could be really needed.

The operation of repairing a deficiency in a metallic
currency would be of the simplest; we have experience to guide us. A scarcity of silver—at least
it was so before railways came into existence—frequently occurs in particular districts of England.
Shopkeepers are embarrassed to give change; farmers
are puzzled how to pay wages; millowners dread
Saturday night; every one who seeks change for
a sovereign is in a difficulty. A paucity of gold is
soon remedied : the local banks quickly get supplies
from London, and London can replenish itself from
abroad, if only, as Adam Smith remarks, London has
the wherewithal to pay for it. A dearth of silver
is more perplexing : railway companies and other
collectors of silver are pressed not to send away their
receipts, and the expense of fetching silver from other
districts has to be endured. But no one talks of
bankruptcy, of loss of property, much less of universal ruin : there is a social inconvenience for the
moment, and a little cost and trouble soon sets all
straight. Sometimes a premium is given for a bag
of silver. The same process would go on upon a
larger scale for gold. The Bank of France recently
thought its metallic reserve insufficient; it had
no difficulty in buying a couple of millions' worth
from London. Recourse would be had to endless

expedients to diminish the temporary inconvenience. People would not pay their tradesmen's bills till they were large enough to be settled by a cheque: cheques would be rapidly multiplied; postage-stamps would come largely into play, as in America. By such appliances the deficiency of one particular instrument of exchange would be remedied, and the business of life would proceed as usual. If the exportation continued, some expense no doubt would have to be incurred in getting a supply from abroad: the payment of a penny or two per sovereign would make gold rush in from every reservoir in the world. But is there any greater misfortune in having to pay a little higher price for one's gold than for one's wool or cotton? That has not been shown, and never can be shown.

You will observe that I deal with the question as one of mere currency. I assume that gold is deficient, but also—and this is very important—that there are means, property, wherewith to purchase the gold. If there are not, if it is the means that fail, the whole matter becomes instantly changed. The question becomes one, not in the least of currency, but of means, of capital, and then it is quite possible that a loss of coin might be very hard indeed to recover.

I am perfectly aware of the answer which will be given me. I shall be told that an export of gold diminishes the coin, and thereby makes the reserves of banks to dwindle down; that the bankers then become uneasy, and in order to restore their reserves feel reluctant to lend; that they then raise their rates of discount, to the great injury of trade; that merchants reply by withdrawing their deposits from the banks, alarm spreads, and ultimately generates panic; and that then the export of gold, acting on the currency, inflicts fearful disasters on the whole community. To this I answer, that even admitting these statements to be true—an admission which I do not make—they would amount to this, and to this only: that the business of a banker places him in such a position towards the currency, that its fluctuations act upon him more than upon other traders. They do not touch the nature and operations of currency, nor require us to believe that there is something peculiar and exceptional in its action compared with other commodities. They only declare that banks are specially affected by what is going on in the gold trade. But it is the same with other trades. A merchant in wool, cotton, or indigo, is peculiarly accessible to the changes which occur in these commodities; but he does not, like the banker, preach that the wool or cotton trade is unlike all other trades. However, currency, and more especially paper currency, is so mixed up with banking, that it is desirable to examine the nature and functions of a bank before we address ourselves to the second division of our subject, Paper Money; and this I propose to do in my following lecture.

LECTURE III.

OUR investigation has now explained, I trust, the nature and action of a metallic currency. Gold in the form of money or coin is simply a commodity employed for bartering, as a ship for carrying or a plough for farming. It is a commodity like any other: in no way distinguished from them except by its own particular qualities, as wood is distinguished from iron by its own peculiar nature. It is selected for bartering for the sole reason that its qualities fit it for this purpose, just as wool is an excellent material for clothing. It obeys the general laws which govern all commodities: it possesses no exceptional features beyond the properties imparted to it by nature. In the form of coin it is useful for bartering only. The value of coin consists solely in the usefulness of the work it performs. It is not sought for its own sake as an article of consumption, but purely as a machine. It is not wealth to its owner till it does its work, till it is parted with and procures commodities. It is wealth only in the identical sense that a cart is;

F

for its action is very similar to a cart's: it fetches for its owner the things he is in want of. Or, to change the figure, 'a guinea,' says Adam Smith, 'may be considered as a bill for a certain quantity of necessaries and conveniences upon all the tradesmen in the neighbourhood.' It is nothing but machinery, and must never be regarded as valuable, except for the work it performs, so long as it remains in the state of coin. It can be converted at pleasure into an end, into an article of consumption, by being sold as metal: till then it is a mere tool, and wealth only in the sense that tools are wealth. Its specific worth, the work for which money is made, is to supersede single by double barter: for the exchanges which are indispensable to civilized life could not be carried on by direct barter. Selling is the first half of double barter; the second half is obtained when the coin got by the sale is itself sold for something else. Whenever gold buys, it is also itself sold: the goods and the gold fare exactly alike in every sale and every purchase. Men take money in selling solely in order to sell that money again in buying. Two great advantages are thus obtained. First, division of labour becomes possible, because a seller is not obliged to wait till he can find a customer who is in want of the particular article he has made. Secondly, a common measure of value is supplied by money for estimating the worth of every commodity, value meaning the quantity of gold which each commodity will fetch. This measure of value gold furnishes, not by its peculiar qualities as a metal, but solely by its intrinsic worth, that is, by its cost of production. A sale for money is an exchange of two equal costs of production, omitting rarity and

other exceptional circumstances. This is the reason
why other articles can serve as currency besides gold
or silver—because the intrinsic worth of the article
for which goods are sold is the essential point of a
purchase. Gold and silver, however, have been preferred, on account of their convenience, and of their
cost of production being supposed to be little liable
to fluctuation. Like every other article, gold is
subject to the law of supply and demand : at a given
time the supply may be deficient or excessive ; there
may be too much money as well as too little money
in a country. When there is too much gold it is
found that merchants export it, and it is a great
advantage that they send it away to procure things
which are wanted and can be used. If it is deficient
for the work it has to do, so that change becomes
scarce, a supply is purchased from abroad by sending
out goods to purchase it. In trade at home it pays
debts ; it does the same in the foreign trade, by paying
the balance due to a foreign country which does not
buy as much of English goods as England has purchased of its merchandize. This payment of a foreign
debt may at times cause a considerable export of
gold ; and thus some cost and trouble—still to a
really unimportant extent—may be incurred in getting
back a supply to fill up any deficiency which may
have been created. The machinery of banking may
throw a large part of this inconvenience on a particular class, on bankers : and under the pressure of
this personal inconvenience the bankers have widely
spread the notion that the burden thus brought upon
their business is a peril for the whole community.
They proclaim it to be the source of every kind of
commercial calamity. In tracing therefore the effects

which a deficient supply of currency might produce,
it becomes necessary to have a clear understanding
of the nature of a bank: and this necessity will be
felt yet more strongly when I come to speak of the
second part of my subject, of Paper Currency and
Banknotes.

I will now put the question in its most absolute
form : What is a bank ? What is the nature of its
functions ? In what does it deal ? It deals in money,
every one will exclaim ; but this is not so. I am
speaking of banks which do not issue notes : it is
desirable to postpone banks of issue to the head of
Paper Currency. An ordinary bank does not deal in
money, in cash, in sovereigns and banknotes. A
bank handles very little cash, very few sovereigns
and notes, compared with the amount of its business.
People naturally associate the idea of money with
a bank. We all get the money we use from our
bankers. When a man speaks of getting a supply
of money, all the world understands that he is thinking of his banker. There are cashiers at every bank
who spend the day in receiving and paying money ;
and this seems to be the only business going on
inside of a bank. A bank and money are inseparable
ideas ; nevertheless, I repeat, money is not the business
of a bank, it is not a dealer in money. Sir John
Lubbock will furnish us with a very clear and decisive
proof of the truth of this assertion. He has given us
the analysis of a sum of 19,000,000*l.* paid in to his
bank in the City :—

Cheques and Bills	.		.	£18,395,000.
Notes	.	.	.	.	487,000.
Coin	.	.	.	.	118,000.

Three per cent. only of the whole amount were paid
in in cash, and coin constituted only one-half per cent.,
or 1 in 200, of the entire sum. Sir John Lubbock's
bank, then, has not cash for its staple. If that bank
ever does anything for trade, it is not with sovereigns
and notes that it does it. It handles cash, no doubt,
but so does every trader and every man in the
country. To use money gives no indication of a
man's business. Every one has to buy, and every
one has to pay: a banker, in that respect, is only just
like all his neighbours. Those cashiers, with their
notes and sovereigns and scales, are only the hands
with which a banker handles his small change; they
tell us nothing about Sir John Lubbock's business
or its nature. We must think of something else
than money if we wish to discover what is the
business which a banker carries on. We must look
to the one big item in his statement—that item
which makes up 97 per cent. of his receipts, of the
things he gets. Here we shall find his staple, the
article he deals in; and that article is cheques and
bills. What, then, are these cheques and bills?
We have learnt what coin is; we have become acquainted with a metallic currency and its nature:
but what are cheques and bills, which make up the
banking trade? Many would say they are papers
which represent money; but I cannot accept the
word 'represent' in currency, for I can never understand its meaning. It has no definite meaning for
me, nor, as far as I can perceive, for any one else.
Anyhow, cheques and bills are not money. They
may, in their respective spheres, do the same work as
money; but in this place, where we are speaking of a
purely metallic currency, they plainly are not money.

What are they, then? Orders to pay money, which
can be legally enforced; title-deeds to money, which
lead directly to the obtaining of money, but are no
more money than the accounts in a shopkeeper's
books are money. They are all warrants or evidences
of debt: each has got a debt beneath it: they are all
simple declarations to a banker or merchant, 'You
owe me money; pay it in such or such a way, or
to such and such a person.' A cheque on a banker
implies a debt due by the banker as its basis: a bill
is an admission of the acceptor that he owes money
and an undertaking to pay it on a particular day.
Here, then, we have the things a banker deals in, the
resources of which he disposes. Bankers deal in
debts, and a bank is an institution for the transfer of
debts. Bankers deal in orders to pay money in
discharge of debts. Their customers give them these
claims to collect—that is, their coupons, their dividend
warrants, the cheques they may have received—and
the bankers undertake to collect them and get them
paid. So far, a banker's business is identical with
that of a clerk sent round by a great shop to collect
its bills: and so far our bankers have not touched
any money worth mentioning. If they handle money,
it must be when they gather up the payments of
these cheques and bills: from their customers they
got only 3*l.* in 100*l.* of money. But in collecting
these payments, do they demand that these bills and
cheques shall be paid in money, in cash, as they might
legally require? Nothing of the kind: they get no
more money from the payment of these cheques and
bills than they did from the customers who sent them
in. Then how does Sir John Lubbock get paid?
I am speaking of the City—at the Clearing House.

In money? No, not a shilling passes. Every City banker, instead of sending the bills and cheques to the people who have to pay them, sends them to the clearing house. Here clerks make out how many cheques each banker has sent in for payment, and how many have been sent in by the other bankers against him: a balance is struck, and the small resulting payment is made by the banker who has more to pay than to receive giving a cheque for the difference on the Bank of England.

So much for a banker's receipts: he does not obtain them in money; they come to him as cheques and bills. These are his resources. He has much at his command if he gets many cheques and bills; he has little if he has received few. The all-important question is how these cheques and bills are born into the world, what it is that makes a banker have few or many of them at different times? People are ever saying that the banks have much or little money; that money is abundant or scarce. This is very erroneous and very misleading language. Money, cash, sovereigns and banknotes vary very little indeed. Compared with the amount of business going on, with the quantity of loans granted and paid, money is really too insignificant to be worth thinking about. The language should be—bills and cheques, or, if an abstract word is preferred, deposits are scarce or abundant: many cheques and bills have arrived at the bank to-day: it will lend freely, and charge a low rate for its loans. How, then, do these cheques and bills come into existence? Omitting accommodation bills, which are foreign to this discussion, cheques and bills are the offspring of sales; they denote goods bought and paid for, either by a

transfer of a debt or by a promise to pay later.
Every man who gives a cheque has previously
sold something and charged his banker to get the
payment for him; and then in turn he buys something, and orders his banker to pay for it with what
the banker now owes him. The banker's power to
lend to others, his resources, his means, depend
entirely on his customer buying less than he sold:
the banker thus obtains the difference, which he uses
in lending, or in any other way that he likes. If,
secondly, the customer buys as much as he sells, if
he is a man who spends all his income, and leaves no
profits, he will draw as many cheques on his banker
to be paid as he gave him cheques to receive. The
banker obtains no increase of means. If, thirdly, the
customer buys more than he sells, if he makes losses
in business or lives beyond his income, the balance
now falls the other way: the banker finds that more
cheques are drawn upon him than are sent in to him
to collect payment for: his means are reduced; he
is less able to lend: he makes difficulties about loans;
the rate of discount rises, and the City, which has
never investigated the matter, screams in astonishment or indignation. Money, coin and banknotes
have no part in this matter, except as small change.
All the buying and selling, all the borrowing and
lending, takes place by exchanging debts; actual
payment is so rare as not to be worth considering.
'Give me your oil-cake,' says a farmer, 'and I will
tell my banker to pay you.' Does he make an actual
payment? No: the cake-merchant gives the cheque
to his own banker, and forthwith proceeds to buy
linseed, and tells the Russian, in turn, 'I will tell my
banker to pay you.' And so it goes on in every

trade. The resources of a bank all come from sales
of commodities, in which the seller does not buy as
much as he sells, and places at the bank the power
of obtaining the difference. If a farmer's waggon
brings back to the farm commodities of equal value
with the wheat which it carried into the town, there
is nothing for a bank; but if, on the contrary, the
farmer who has brought 50*l.* worth of wheat into
the town, buys only 30*l.* worth of other goods, then
he is still possessed of the power of buying 20*l.*
worth more, and this power, this faculty of purchasing he deposits at the bank, and these are the
funds of which the bank disposes.

We see then what a banker receives: he receives
debts. What does he do with them? How does
he obtain the profits of his trade? The process is
always in substance as follows :—A farmer sells corn :
he gives his landlord a cheque for rent; the landlord
gives the cheque to his country banker: it travels
up to London, and finds its way (not this identical
cheque, but other cheques which it gave birth to)
to the Discount Office of the Bank of England. The
bank finds itself able to lend, because it has found
that it has received debts to collect. An Australian
merchant presents himself: he has a bill due by
the owner of a cargo of wool, but which will not be
paid for three months. He wishes to send off beer
that day to Australia. He asks the bank to take
his bill, and give him the power of drawing cheques
for beer. The bank having debts, I say, to collect,
consents : the beer is bought, and is paid for by
a cheque on the bank, which transfers the debts
it received from the country to the brewer. In this
manner the corn of the farmer is exchanged for the

beer of the brewer : all the rest is machinery, changes
of ownership, of power to buy, but the only realities
in the affair are the corn and the beer. The bank
makes a charge for lending to the Australian merchant on his bill, and this is its profit. The corn
buys the beer ; and the gigantic trades of modern
nations are only this process many times repeated.

I have said that a banker deals in debts, for such
are cheques and bills, but I might have said with
equal truth that a bank deals in power to buy, in
purchasing power. Such is a debt ; for a tradesman
or a manufacturer will let you have his goods in
exchange for a good debt as readily as for money.
The farmer, by the sale of his corn, acquires the
means of buying : he does not buy himself, he lodges
this power to buy with his banker, and gives an
order by a cheque for the transfer of this power
to his landlord. The landlord passes it on—and it
travels through many stages till it reaches the
Australian merchant who buys the beer. The quantity of this buying power, held by the bankers of
England, amounts to hundreds of millions. They
can buy to that extent, but, in other words, it means
that they hold that quantity of debts in their hands.
Who owe these debts? I ask. Of what is this buying power composed? These debts are due by those
who possess the commodities of the country, who own
shops, warehouses, houses, ships, and so on. They
own this property subject to the collective amount of
these debts. They owe these debts to the bankers,
or those to whom the bankers may have transferred
them. The funds of bankers may be rightly regarded
as mortgages on the stock of wealth in the country.
Those in whose hands is this wealth deal with it

as traders at their pleasure; but they are not complete proprietors, they may be called upon by the bankers to surrender a portion of these commodities, precisely as the bankers themselves may be summoned to do the same by their customers. Thus the whole business of banking is occupied with debts, debts registered on pieces of paper and in lines in account-books, debts which possess the power to obtain money, but which power is not exercised beyond the extent of 3 parts in 100. Like their neighbours, bankers pay and receive a very small portion of their debts in money, their business lies with claims for money, embodied in all sorts of papers.

It follows from this examination of the nature of a banker's means, that bankers possess very little capital. The language of the day ascribes the possession of large capital to banks: it describes borrowers as obtaining capital from banks. Even scientific writers, such as Mr. Patterson, speak of the invisible capital held by banks: others dwell with great emphasis on incorporeal wealth, as the key for the explanation of paper currency. This is a profound error in Political Economy. Incorporeal property, such as a right to present a clergyman to a living, or a right of way, is not wealth, though it may readily be sold for wealth. The clergyman presented gets the wealth, but the patron gets nothing else than the nomination of one clergyman rather than another. Yet on the doctrine that incorporeal property is wealth, Mr. Macleod has raised a vast and baseless superstructure of currency. Nor am I acquainted with any form of invisible capital, except the skill and other mental properties of labourers, if even these are to be accounted invisible and not rather integral portions of the compound being, the man who possesses them. A bank possesses no capital beyond the coin in its till and its house with the furniture contained in it. Capital is not what a bank deals in or lends : it cannot lend what it does not possess. What it has to give is the right and power to buy capital, the command of capital, means to go into shops and warehouses and to carry away their goods. It bestows this power by transferring the right to demand gold. The gold, as I have so often said, seldom passes, is seldom seen or heard of ; but sellers instantaneously bow before a well-ascertained right to demand the gold, and furnish their goods as freely to the owner of this right as if he held out to them his hands full of gold.

Wealth and that which will exchange for wealth are not convertible terms in political economy. A man will give a guinea to hear a fine concert : the guinea is wealth, and passes from the hands of the purchaser of the ticket to those of the singer ; but the hearing of the voice is not wealth. A house with a fine view or in a fashionable street will sell or let for more than a precisely similar house which does not command the view or possess the fashion ; but the view is not wealth, neither is the fashion. The owner of the better-situated house may acquire more wealth when he sells or lets it ; but, so long as he dwells in it himself, he is neither richer nor poorer than the possessor of the similar but less favoured house. The same distinction applies to banknotes, bills, cheques, and other forms of property expressed on pieces of paper. The bits of paper are

not wealth or capital; but they are capable of
bringing riches by the evidence they furnish of a
debt due, and by the certainty that they can set the
courts of law in motion to enforce the payment of
that debt. One may hear every day men speaking
of a bank possessing a million in the funds; but the
expression is most inaccurate. The fact spoken of
is, not that the bank has a million of pounds lodged
in the funds, as it might have in a strong chest, but
that it gave some persons a million of pounds for
the right of obtaining 3*l.* a-year so many times over.
This yearly dividend is the sole material fact in
the thing purchased, the only wealth; the million
is the consideration given to the owners of this
right to induce them to transfer it to the bank.
It is easy to give a proof that the bank does not
in any sense possess a million of pounds. This
supposed million is made larger or smaller every
day according as the price of consols varies in the
market; and if England were conquered, and the
National Debt repudiated by the conquerors, the
dividends would cease to be paid, and no buyer
would give anything at all to the bank for the
million which figured in its books. The million
would be entirely expunged from existence; it would
be a worthless asset of the same kind as those which
are often seen on the credit-side of the accounts of
bankrupt companies.

The question now arises, Why, then, do bankers
raise such commotion about currency and banknotes and sovereigns, and count up the quantities
of these things moving about, and use mysterious
and alarming words about the circulation, and
clamour for endless contrivances for controlling it,

as if it were for them something more than the
small change which it is for the rest of the world?
Why should they be more uneasy than other folk?
There is not an unprotected debtor in the kingdom
who might not be suddenly called upon to pay his
debt in cash; and however rich or solvent these
debtors might be, it is certain that by no possibility
could they all find the money at the same hour on the
same day. The richest men might be arrested—yet
we all go about without raising cries of alarm about
the circulation. Nevertheless, there is a substantial
difference in this matter to the disadvantage of the
banker. A rich man suddenly pressed for cash would
seldom suffer inconvenience, it would be merely the
perplexity of a want of change. A rich merchant
might, on the other hand, be exposed to loss and
even disaster, but that would come from the deficiency
of available means at the moment to buy money with
and not from a deficiency of money itself. A merchant's resources are usually locked up for the time,
but the banker's business has one great and fundamental peculiarity. He receives debts from his
customers on the express condition of repaying them
on demand, and that condition is enforced literally,
in hard money, at all hours of the day. He is bound
to produce the money immediately. If he fails, he
commits an act of bankruptcy; his credit, the confidence accorded to him, is destroyed; every one
demands his money, and the bank is ruined. It
is only 3*l*. in 100*l*. which he has got to find in ordinary times; but it might happen that 6*l*. should
be asked for under particular circumstances, and
though he has the 94*l*. placed out in excellent bills,
he might find it very difficult to produce the 6*l*.

This is a danger from which no bank, not even the Bank of England, can ever be absolutely free. If the French came to London, it would not be 6*l.* but more than 60*l.* in ringing metal, which not only its note-holders, but all who bank with the Bank of England, would demand for every 100*l.* due by the bank. On Black Friday in 1866, after the stoppage of the great house of Overend and Gurney, the alarm was so great in the City that no bank felt perfectly sure that its customers might not at once withdraw their accounts; and if they had done so, it is certain that every bank must have stopped. There was not, there could not be, by any human contrivance, money enough to pay every one on that day.

It is natural, therefore, that bankers should be sensitive about the supply of money, that is, of that legal tender which the law requires them to produce at the moment. But the danger, though theoretically possible, has no practical reality outside of the imagination. Insurance companies might just as rationally fall into a panic, that every one was going to die to-day. It is possible, undoubtedly; but every one would see in such a case the exaggeration of fear. Mercantile crises never have their origin in a deficiency of currency, of coin, and notes of legal tender. In the very worst, in 1847, in 1866, no banker who had saleable property, and therefore the means of buying sovereigns and notes, was or could have been under any difficulty to procure them. There never is a conspiracy, or combination, if you will, on the part of the public to hoard every note and sovereign in the country. No banker who had consols to sell, and would have consented to sell at

70*l.* instead of 90*l.*, would have had the smallest
difficulty in getting money. There might be difficulty
about selling consols, for it by no means follows that
the man who possesses sovereigns should wish to
buy consols with them ; that is a consideration quite
distinct from any deficiency of actual coin or money.
The quantity of money required by the public from
the bankers for use is a matter of average, just as the
number of deaths for an Assurance Office. Sometimes
more is wanted, sometimes less ; but the limits of
variation are very narrow compared with the mass
of payments effected. On Black Friday in 1866 more
actual money was needed, because many accounts were
transferred in banknotes from one bank to another,
and bankers all over the country, from prudence,
increased their stock of banknotes ; but still there was
enough, a full and ample supply ; that is, I repeat,
no one who had property that could be sold failed
to procure sovereigns or notes. That is the only
true test of the fact whether the supply was sufficient or not.

It will not do to say, what is so incessantly
repeated in commercial circles, that money was so
dreadfully scarce that actually advances could not
be obtained from the Bank of England, or other
banks, on the security of consols or silver. Worse
logic cannot be imagined ; the conclusion has no root
in the premises. The two statements are unconnected
by any law of reasoning. The word ' money ' is used
here for loans of money, and even then, not loans
to be made over the counter in coin, but loans
merely reckoned in money but for the most part
taken out in cheques. The refusal of the bank to
make advances did not show that currency was

scarce, because if they had been granted, they would
not have been given in money; it proves rather that
lending was very difficult for the bank, no matter
what the security offered was. A lender on the
security of consols or silver, or of a mortgage on land,
is practically a buyer for the time of silver and land :
is it pretended that the Bank of England, or all the
banks of the world put together, with all the gold of
the world at their command, could buy on a given
day all the land of England ? What if all the mass
of consols, the whole National Debt had been offered
to the bank as a security for an advance, does any
sane man suppose that the bank could have made
such a loan, and that if it refused, it was because
coin and banknotes were deficient ? The very statement of the questions shows how ridiculous they
are ; and yet they only embody the idea of the
multitudes who cried out in 1866, and cry out still,
that loans were made difficult, and merchants injured,
by a restricted circulation, as they call it. There is
no connection whatever between the goodness of a
security and the ability to lend, as every one finds
out in daily life. Every day people are obliged
to sell valuable property at a sacrifice, because they
cannot find lenders : but the theory of the City
is, that the bank ought to be a universal and in-
exhaustible lender. Such nonsense could not live
were it not for the sonorous words with which
it is expressed. Lending, the lending of trade and
banks, is not made with money, whether coin or
notes ; and the stock of money has nothing to do
with it. There is, as I have said, but one true
test of a scarcity of gold, as of every other commodity,—that buyers who have the means to pay

for it, cannot procure it. Shillings have often been scarce, and people who had to pay large sums for wages have at times been forced to give a premium for a bag of shillings ; but when does a buyer of sovereigns—not in a banker's parlour, but in a bullion-dealer's shop — with adequate means to purchase, fail to procure them, or is obliged to pay more than twenty shillings for each of them ?

The way to try the question is not to offer consols to a bank for a loan, but to sell the consols and then to see whether you cannot get gold with the proceeds. Oh, but consols could not be sold on Black Friday! Could they not? If they had been offered for sale at half their value one might have seen whether they could not have been sold. The sacrifice and loss would have been dreadful, no doubt; but what has this loss to do with the supply of gold, any more than with the supply of tea and timber? The question, then, is whether currency, sovereigns, and notes were scarce ; and manifestly the terrible sacrifice incurred by a banker or a merchant who has debts to pay, and must sell whatever property he has, is no proof whatever that there were not plenty of notes and sovereigns to be had. The price of consols, or of any other property, depends on buyers being found to purchase ; and it does not follow that a man who has 10,000 sovereigns should be at all disposed to buy consols or any other particular thing. Who that has a good horse to sell does not know the difficulty of getting a price at all equal to its value, if he is obliged to sell suddenly on an emergency ? He may be surrounded by men of immense fortunes, and not averse too to buying a good horse, yet how seldom

does such a seller get the worth of his horse. But
he does not cry out that there is a deficiency of gold
or of currency in the country : it is the City and
the City articles alone, who think that they are
different from other people, and that what happens
to them is not the same as what happens to others.
The City forgets that gold and notes are wanted
only for those payments which are made with these
tools, and that loans and advances do not employ
currency. Mercantile borrowers get their loans by
sums placed to their credit, which they draw out
with cheques.   They pay their creditors with
cheques, they carry on their business with cheques,
cheques do all the work, at least 97 parts out of
100. Borrowing and lending may vary enormously
as to ease or difficulty, without a single additional
sovereign or note being set in motion. Every one
must see that it is so who understands the nature
of money and the nature of a bank. You have learnt
that the farmer's corn was exchanged for the brewer's
beer without the intervention of a single sovereign
or note ; it was done by means of bits of paper,
by orders to pay. Banks were set to work, the
operations of trade were made larger, a discount
or two was earned, money, in the inaccurate and
perverse commercial sense, was made cheaper by
the sale of the corn, and yet a barter of corn for
beer was the only reality in the whole affair. All
the rest was pure machinery for exchanging, a machinery of paper. The power of that paper lay
in the words written upon it, words which the law
will compel, if required, to be made good, orders
to pay gold, but which gold, as you have seen,
is never paid at all.

But bankers will reply: This is all very well; but all the world knows that his reserve is the vital point for a banker; that its importance is recognized to be so great that the law compels the greatest of banks, the Bank of England, to publish the state of its reserve every week; that the commercial world is comfortable or anxious according as the reserve is going up or down; and that all reserves are composed of cash, of currency, of sovereigns and bank-notes. Every one of these assertions is true; and yet they furnish no countenance whatever to the delusion that the business of either bankers or merchants depends on the quantity of currency afloat in the country. A little examination of the nature of a banker's reserve will make this clear. A banker's business consists of three parts: debts which the banker has received from his customers, and which he is liable to be called upon to repay; secondly, debts which he has granted to others and which they are bound to repay him at the time which he has stipulated for; and thirdly, a fund of cash, called his reserve, which he keeps in hand to meet such payments as are demanded in cash. A banker receives from one set of people and lends to another set of people; and a perfect bank would be one which received and paid or lent exactly the same sums every day. That is the ideal of the banking business, and no doubt every sound bank does its best to attain to this condition. Under such circumstances, the reserve would be steady; it would not alter, it would become merely a safeguard against exceptional fluctuations which no intelligence could foresee.

Now how is such a happy condition to be

reached? Nay, can it be reached at all? It can
be conceived as existing only in the case of a bank
whose customers consisted of persons of fixed incomes, who received their funds in well-known and
regular amounts, never exceeded their means, and
drew them out at regular intervals; and further,
which could place its deposits in investments always
perfectly saleable without loss. But such a bank
is not to be found in England. The funds of every
bank are largely derived from trade, and are un-
avoidably exposed to all the fluctuations of trade;
and consequently the equilibrium of receipts and
payments becomes a matter demanding high intelligence and skill from every banker. His reserve
must vary: at times it will vary enormously: and
as it must always be sufficient to avert a stoppage
of the bank by being able to meet every demand
for payment, it is natural that the banker should be
very sensitive about it and watch its movements
with a very jealous eye. He must study the causes
which produce these movements; for how can he
lend or invest his resources to-day, resources which
he may be called upon at any moment to return
to those who supplied him with them, unless he
makes a forecast of the probabilities of to-morrow?
His reserve is composed of cash, of gold and notes,—
and when he finds his customers drawing out their
accounts, and the reserve diminishing rapidly, what
more obvious, what more natural, than to exclaim
that there are too few notes and too little gold in
the country, and that this is the reason why his
reserve is diminishing? Give England more gold,
cry her bankers, and then we shall have our reserves
replenished: Get more gold into circulation, re-echo

trembling merchants, and then the bankers will lend
us money and discount our bills freely and cheaply.
Alas! I fear that the problem which always lies before
the banker is far harder than the City and the newspapers fancy it to be, and is not to be solved by so
easy a nostrum. The reserve is dwindling away, because the receipts which feed it are diminishing; and
Sir John Lubbock tells us that gold figures in these
receipts for only one two-hundredth part. It is
positively absurd to speak of a variation of the stock
of gold in England, a variation which, in a month or
even year, can never be but trifling compared with
the whole mass in circulation—to describe, I say,
such a variation as being the prime cause of the
diminution of a fund, of which it constitutes only
one part in 200. Such a doctrine is an absurdity
on the very face of it; and yet this is the explanation, this the language, which is given by many
bankers, and great merchants, and solemn authorities
in Parliament, whenever the banking trade falls into
trouble, and traders find discount very dear or even
impossible to obtain.

The banker must carry his studies into a very
different region if he desires to understand the forces
which act upon his reserve. He must look at his
receipts and his loans, for they are the things he
deals in; he must try to learn the causes which
influence their movements. It is by adjusting the
one to the other—what he lends to what he receives—
that he maintains his reserves. Unfortunately for the
banker, his knowledge is often of necessity conjec-
tural, and his control over both very limited. There
is one way indeed in which he can always with
certainty maintain his reserve and be perfectly safe:

he can keep what he receives, and neither lend nor invest it; but this is to extinguish his profits and to kill his business. The next thing he may do is to lend in such a way as to be able to get it back immediately. This all bankers would like to do: but it is impossible, for they could not find the means of placing out all their resources on such terms: and moreover, such a system would prevent them from assisting trade by discounting bills, and would strip banking of most of its value. The result, then, is that a considerable portion of banking loans cannot be recovered on the spur of the moment: and as most banking deposits may be demanded and drawn out suddenly and without notice, we reach the great danger which is inherent in all banking, and can never be quite got rid of—the danger that customers may claim their deposits and accounts at a time when the banker cannot procure back his means from those to whom he has lent them. It is this never-absent danger which renders a banker so sensitive about his reserve: for the danger first reveals itself in the diminution of the reserve, of the fund in hand for making payments.

We see, then, the supreme importance for a banker that he should at all times know the influences which are acting on the persons who have lodged their funds in his hands — that he should understand what is likely to happen to his receipts, to those cheques and bills which constitute 97 parts out of 100 of the sums which he has received and which he owes to others on demand. The foolish talk about gold and notes is only too apt to mislead him, and to divert his attention from the points he ought to study, from the causes which

are at work amongst his depositors. The reserve
shows signs of diminishing—his creditors are claiming
back their money faster than his debtors are repaying
him their loans—what is he to study and to watch?
Not the worthless statistics about the number of
sovereigns and notes in circulation, but the state of the
wealth of the nation, the forces which are increasing
or diminishing it. This is what he will ponder over,
if he knows that his resources proceed from sales of
wealth, of commodities, and that they are composed
of a power of buying again, acquired by the sellers
from their purchases, and which they have not
entirely used up by buying as much as they have
sold. But how many bankers, how many merchants
and traders possess this knowledge? How many are
aware that 97 parts out of 100 of their means imply
that commodities have been sold to buyers, and that
the sellers have not bought other commodities to
the full value of those they sold? How many are
conscious that the vital matter for them is that
commodities should increase, or at least not diminish;
and that the sellers of goods should not immediately
at the time buy as much as they sell? If a farmer,
I repeat, has a good harvest, he acquires a profit by
the sale of his corn: and if his waggon does not
bring back from the town goods worth as much as
the sacks of wheat it carried in, the farmer's power
of buying is not exhausted, and he has something to
place at a banker's. If, on the contrary, the harvest
has been ruined by rain, and has not replaced the
cost of cultivating the land, the farmer has incurred
a loss, and probably must withdraw some of the
funds which he had lodged with the banker. This
is the universal type of the relation which a bank

bears to its resources, whether it be a farmer, or
a merchant who has got an account at the bank;
and thus we see what it is that a banker has to
explore and judge—the movements of the national
wealth.

It is hard, beyond doubt, to investigate so vast
a field in the actual life of modern England; but
on no other tenure is safe banking or safe trading
possible. It is easy to reckon up banknotes issued,
or to count the ingots in the cellars of the bank,
and then to exult in the swelling numbers, and to
make large loans to traders, and to send orders for
costly cargoes of merchandize to distant lands: but
what if autumnal rains in England, or early frosts
in cotton regions, or civil strife in America, or barren
silkworms in France or Italy, or some gigantic unproductive consumption of war anywhere, have
destroyed wealth, and failed to restore the consumption effected by cultivation, and have impoverished the world, and lessened the means of foreigners
to buy in England, and diminished capital, and so
loans have become difficult and the rate of discount
flies upward? What will it avail to say, that when
the bank extended its loans, and merchants sent out
their orders, they relied on the quantity of banknotes circulating, and the store of metal reposing in
the vaults, and had inferred that they were safe in
making engagements because the large circulation
guaranteed strong reserves for banks and low rates
of interest for traders? Will the sovereigns be found
in the banker's reserves, when impoverished traders
on every side have not only not supplied fresh
means to bankers, but have been compelled to take
away from them the funds which they had been

went to leave in their hands? Think of one disturbing force alone. Many Englishmen have been
compelled to live on reduced incomes, and not a
few have passed into bankruptcy, solely from the
action of men who live thousands of miles away.
The Americans broke out into civil war, and cotton
almost ceased to be grown in America. How many
calculated its effects upon England? how many in
discussing the disasters of 1866 gave a single thought
to America? Yet the recoil of that great event told
severely on the City and the money-market. Banks
had fewer accounts, and those still left were smaller,
for many of their customers had lost their means.
The trade with America no longer yielded its ancient
profits: the Americans bought less of England,
because they produced less at home; and with the
diminution of trade and profit, banking resources
dwindled away. It is owing to events like these
that a banker's reserve shows signs of failing, and
requires to be fed by the sale of investments entail-
ing perhaps a gigantic loss: that the banker wants
gold to pay the ever-increasing difference between
the demands made upon him and the sums he can
collect from his creditors: and that at last a universal
cry for more gold breaks forth from every office in
the whole City.

But is this cry reasonable? Whilst the merchant
and the banker are thus agonized to get money, the
bullion-shop over the way is overflowing with the
metal. The banker can obtain it instantly, if he can
pay for it; but the pinch lies there. He urgently
needs gold: but it is not gold that fails, but, as
Adam Smith long ago remarked, the means wherewithal to buy it.

The cause of the banker's need is the movement amongst borrowers and lenders, amongst bills and cheques. It is capital which is in disorder all around, not gold. In the worst crises gold is always to be had, but not the loan of gold. Loans are dearer, but gold remains stationary in value. Its buying power in relation to land and property outside the financial world continues unchanged. The prices of some commodities may fall; but then that happens because many persons have become poorer, and can no longer afford to consume and buy : or because the dealers in these commodities are obliged to make forced sales in stagnant or depreciated markets. All these are questions of capital, and in no respect of currency. In seasons of panic, bankers and traders desire the gold to be in their own hands, and it is in the hands of the other members of the community, and that is all.

But again, I shall be told, that whatever political economists may say, hard facts demonstrate that when a drain of gold sets in for exportation the rate of discount has a tendency to rise. That combination of the two events is undoubtedly frequent; but it admits of a very natural and easy explanation. The export of gold indicates that England has bought more abroad than she has sold ; the difference has to be paid in gold. When a nation buys more than it sells, it fares like individual men ; the excess must come out of spare funds, which, in the case of the nation, are for the most part placed in the hands of the bankers. The purchasers of these foreign goods find loans from bankers to be their most available resource ; they draw bills on the security of the goods to arrive ; the bankers discount the bills, either with gold, which is the identical article wanted, or with cheques, which forthwith are used to buy gold. The gold goes abroad, and the bankers have been asked for an unusual quantity of loans. The two events happen together, and are both joint effects of one cause. The rise of discount is not the result of the exportation of gold, but of the increase of purchases, necessitating loans. I have already remarked that such an outflow is of no importance. All the best writers are agreed that a foreign drain, as it is called, never raises a commotion at home worth noticing; the quantity sent away never produces a real scarcity.

On the other hand, many authorities assure us that an internal drain which takes gold from the bankers to be used in the country is often an event of extreme gravity; but we have here only the recurrence of the same confusion between cause and effect. Many more sovereigns are used in summer and autumn than in spring and winter: the event recurs every year, yet one never hears the remark, that discount, as a rule, is dearer in summer than in winter. Winter is not famed for low discounts. No agitation accompanies this annual migration of the gold; and the fact ought to have taught the lesson, that if there is evil, the evil exists in the cause, and not in the mere fact of gold being removed from the banks. Such evil may break forth; and it did come to pass in 1866. In that terrible crisis large sums of gold were withdrawn from the London bankers: but the cause lay in finance, not in currency. Frightened depositors thought their money to be nowhere so safe as in their own keeping, and country bankers fortified their reserves with additional notes. Nevertheless, there was no deficiency of currency, as I shall show hereafter, when we treat of banknotes. There might have sprung up a demand on that day, as I have already observed, which all the currency of the country could not have satisfied: every sovereign due by bankers might have been claimed. The panic did not reach such a height; but if the run had been so violent as to break every bank, what would have been the interpretation of such a disaster? That the currency was deficient? Certainly not; for the words 'sufficiency' and 'deficiency' relate to the average demands of the banking business, with an allowance for variations up and down, and by no means to a possible demand of every debt due. There never can be currency enough for such a demand. No insurance office could pay for the damage which the burning of the whole of London would create. Practical life must rely on fair practical averages; violent and overwhelming excess lies beyond the arrangement which any practical trade can contemplate.

It will be inferred from what precedes that the tendency of a reserve to rise or fall is of greater importance than any variation of its actual figures. The anxious question always is how far the diminution will extend, to what lengths the demands of customers for repayment, and the failures of debtors to fulfil their engagements with the bank, will proceed. The movements of the reserve are therefore most deserving objects of study and watching; but the object to be discovered is not how much currency is moving about, but what are the causes which are acting upon both these classes of persons. These causes belong to the domain of capital exclusively; they relate to buying and selling of commodities, to

influences diminishing wealth, and the like; they have
no connection with currency.

I desire, in conclusion, to point out the immense
economy which that excellent institution a bank
generates in currency. The precious metals are very
costly to purchase, and they entail no trifling loss
from wear and tear in being used; the cheque does
the same work, and costs nothing. Within its own
sphere it buys and sells with equal facility with the
sovereign; and that sphere in England embraces the
largest portion of all the business transacted. The
bank interposes itself between the buyer and the
seller, precisely as the sovereign; it brings the Lincolnshire farmer and the London brewer together, exactly
as the sovereign brought the tailor and the baker. It
is one of the most striking triumphs of modern times
to have invented a machine of such superlative cheapness and efficiency; and it bears the most decisive
evidence to the public order, the sense of security,
the supremacy of law, and the intelligence of the
society in which it is freely used. In combination
with its offspring the clearing-house, it dispenses with
gold and paper currency almost entirely. The cheque
is emphatically an English institution, for it is in little
favour elsewhere, at least in Continental Europe. It
turns an English bank itself into a clearing-house, or
a kind of accountant's office; for the largest number
of English cheques are never paid in money. One
cheque is set off against another, and property is exchanged without the intervention of coin or banknotes.
It is treated with comparative neglect by its banking
parents, for their thoughts are ever set on notes, and
their eyes directed to the movements of gold: yet
the cheque is more powerful, more to be desired or

dreaded than either. It is the cheque which brings riches within the portals of the banker; and the cheque is the fearful instrument on whose wings they take their flight. The numbers of his inferior kinsman, the note, are carefully recorded each recurring week, and traders are taught to regard it as the barometer of the commercial atmosphere; but it is the cheque which constitutes the resources of the banker, and it is the cheque which threatens and often accomplishes his downfall. And yet this mighty potentate is not a payment, but only an order for payment; and the order is seldom literally obeyed. For my part, let others dwell on notes, the numbers of their circulation, their tendency to increase or diminish, their stability and their solvency—let me rather hear of the movements and the operations of the cheque. The rising flood of cheques, as it is a sign of the activity, so also is it the usual mark of the profitableness of business; their ebb too surely announces the drooping resources of commerce. Great is the note, I admit; but far greater yet is the cheque.

LECTURE IV.

PAPER CURRENCY.

I HAVE now reached the second division of my subject, Paper Money. In the preceding lectures we have ascertained the laws and principles which govern a metallic currency, or coin; and we shall find that the same general rules and principles prevail in paper money also, subject only to such modifications of detail as are created by the difference between metal and paper. It will be seen that coin and paper money perform the same work. They are employed for making transfers of property, for carrying out exchanges of commodities; but with this distinction between them, that each has a sphere of action which its peculiar qualities fit it to occupy with greater public advantage than the other. In many operations of buying and selling they both are used indiscriminately, but there are others in which the actual metal with its intrinsic worth is superior to what is a legal engagement only, and not the payment of an actual equivalent.

We have reaped a great advantage from confining

11

our investigation in the first instance to metallic currency. The complications involved in paper currency are more subtle and more difficult to analyse than any found in money composed of coin, and we should have had our path encumbered with endless briars of collateral discussion. We arrived at first principles in the investigation of coin ; our duty is to adhere to them closely, and to apply them firmly, under the conviction that money, currency, whether made of paper or metal, in its leading features is always the same, and that its various forms all work out the same general result.

The cheque has furnished us with a very natural introduction to the discussion of paper money. The cheque has taught us that an obligation to pay coin, a transfer of a debt, a mere order to pay sovereigns will, in by far the largest number of sales and purchases, buy commodities and settle debts as easily and as effectually as sovereigns themselves. In imagination, in hypothesis, the sovereigns are always supposed to be present at every sale, and at every payment, and to be handed over ; but they do not actually pass. The debt, that is, the value of the article which is bought, is always reckoned up in real pounds, shillings, and pence, and the cheque is treated as if it were money itself; but it is not money, but only a request, a command to pay money. The intrinsic worth of the gold, the value of the gold, always is the measure of what any commodity purchased is worth. The thought of the gold and its value, of its power to buy other articles in return for the one delivered over to the buyer, is always present to the minds of both buyer and seller, consciously or unconsciously, in every transaction carried out by paper payment of every kind. To sell, even when the gold cannot possibly be procured, always means to give a commodity in exchange for coin: and even single barter, on a large scale, can scarcely be conceived as possible except upon the supposition that the minds of each of the barterers first estimated in money the values of the things bartered. Nevertheless, the cheque has shown us that the gold needs not to be handled and transferred from one man's hands to another's: and when enormous transactions of trade were found to be settled as conveniently by pieces of paper as they would have been by gold, men quickly perceived how vast was the saving of expense and how immense the convenience gained by substituting the paper for the coin.

The bill of exchange had taught the same lesson as the cheque long before the use of banknotes as money had been invented. The bill, like the cheque, substitutes an undertaking or order to pay for payment itself; differing from the cheque only in respect of certain regulations for its management which peculiarly fit it for certain commercial transactions, more especially for foreign trade. The cheque orders a banker to make a payment of so much money. The man who gives away a horse for a cheque relies on the buyer having that sum of money at his account with the banker: if the banker, on presentation, should declare that the drawer of the cheque has not assets at the bank sufficient to pay the cheque, the seller has lost his horse, and can recover its value only by suing the buyer at law. The bill is armed by law with larger powers. It must be paid on a given day, and the law in all countries gives greater facilities for the recovery of the sum due upon a bill than

upon a like sum claimed as a simple debt. Further,
the bill engages the liability of more persons than
one, for the bills which have only one name are very
rare indeed. A bill, as a rule, has the names of a
drawer and acceptor, and very often of several in-
dorsers besides. Each of these persons is liable to
pay the bill; and thus such an instrument is excellently suited for trading with foreign countries. A
merchant in New York, who sells cotton to be paid
for after the lapse of three months, gains by means
of a bill much greater security than he could have
obtained from a cheque, or a common admission of
debt—he obtains the additional security of every
person whose name is written on the bill. I have
entered into these details for the sake of showing
you, in cases free from the theories and the jargon
with which banknotes have been smothered, the
nature and use of paper money. I do not call
cheques and bills money, for a reason which I shall
state hereafter; but they perform the precise work
of money, each in its own career, namely, the transfer
of the ownership of property from one man to
another, and they are identical with the banknote
on every point except subordinate details.

The use of paper money rests on the fact that men
are willing—for there is no compulsion—to accept
a promise or obligation to pay, a written warrant
of debt, in the place of coin in parting with their
property. The act of accepting this paper is purely
voluntary, just as the acceptance of a sovereign by
a shopkeeper is voluntary. Legal tender has no
voice in the matter, as I shall explain at a later
period. The hatter who consents to give his hat
for a sovereign, and the American who gives away

his cotton for a bill, both act of their own free will.
The latter might have demanded a pair of boots
as the price of his hat, and the American half-a-dozen
locomotives in exchange for his cotton. But, practically, universal experience shows that in civilized
countries credit is voluntarily given, tradesmen re-
lying on the ultimate payment of the accounts when
sent in, and takers of cheques and bills assuming
that these orders will be paid on presentation. There
is seldom any actual payment in either of these processes, any completion of the barter, of the exchange
of equivalent commodities, which is the essence of
every sale ; the second half, the quantity of metal
stipulated, the coin, is pledged and promised, but
it seldom appears at all. The transaction, the
purchases and payments are completed by account ;
one debt is set off against another; the tradesman's
debt and the American's bill are both discharged, in
most cases, by the transfer of a debt due by a banker.

But there is one feature in these modes of exchange
to which I beg your particular attention, for it plays
a prominent part in discussions on banknotes. The
merchant who took the bill has lost his cotton ; the
seller who gave his horse for a cheque will probably
never set eyes on the horse again. Both these persons have given away property, and for the moment,
though holding a cheque and a bill, have received
nothing, no equivalent portion of wealth, in return.
This fact, stated in the reverse form, teaches us that
paper payment of every kind is a contrivance for
obtaining property without furnishing the equivalent
at the time. Issuers, therefore, of paper money are
people who acquire goods and do not pay for them
till the payment of the debt written on the paper

is demanded. So long as the bill is not yet due, whoever holds the bill has so much property the less. No doubt if the bill has a good repute, and the acceptor is held to be solvent, the possessor of the bill in ordinary times can obtain the equivalent property to which the bill gives him a title, for the bill is saleable; it will buy other merchandize, it may be exchanged for money, whether sovereigns or banknotes, or be discounted at some bank. Nevertheless, the truth remains good: whoever has bought the bill has for the time lost wealth; he recovers it only when the bill is paid. For the moment he has a piece of paper, and no other wealth than the intrinsic worth of that piece of paper, that is, nothing at all. That piece of paper is a purchasing power; it can buy, it can procure wealth; but wealth and the power to get wealth are two most different things. The one is a piece of paper only; the other may be a vast estate. This is a consideration of supreme importance for a right understanding of the nature and action of banknotes.

The bill and the cheque in time generated the banknote, which may be regarded as a cheque, payable to the bearer on demand, drawn and signed by the banker upon his own bank. That is its real essence. It is a cheque: and do not forget this truth, like so many great authorities. But observe also that though notes are generally issued by banks, there is no necessary and inseparable connection between notes and banking. I shall show you presently that the greatest of all banknotes, the so-called note of the Bank of England, is not issued by a bank, but by an office of the State. It is true that, practically, notes are issued by banks only, and

for the very plain reason that bankers are better
qualified than any other persons to deal with the
funds procured by the emission of notes. Notes issued by a trader, even by a Baring, would not circulate, for they would inevitably be exposed to all the
risks of his trade. It is the business of a banker to
deal with funds expressed in money, whether in the
form of coin, or of bills and other papers containing
claims for coin: and this business is carried on upon
the understanding that the banker is not to trade,
but to lend out his receipts upon securities of un-
questionable value. To obtain money, or what can
command money, from the public, and then to lend
it out again, is exactly the banker's profession: and
since a banker is universally understood to be bound
not to trade with his receipts, but to place them
out upon securities which completely protect them
from being lost, he is the very man to whom the
public will naturally give their money, or their
power to procure money or money's worth, in return
for his acknowledgments expressed on pieces of
paper or notes. The public will retain and use
these notes as convenient instruments for buying
and selling, precisely because there is an understanding that the funds given to the banker for
them are in perfectly safe keeping: but, on the
contrary, the same public will not retain in circulation a princely merchant's notes, because it knows
that the merchant would trade with the funds, and
there would be but a very imperfect guarantee
against their being lost. It sends in the cheques
of the Barings and the Rothschilds for payment:
it makes use of the notes of a Scotch bank, and
does not send them in for payment. But this acci-

dental, or rather non-essential, connection of notes
with banking is, alas! the parent of interminable
confusion. It is the plague-spot of all currency:
the foreign and insoluble ingredient which will
neither itself crystallize nor suffer the other elements
to crystallize. In and out of Parliament, at home
and abroad, amongst scientific writers and newspaper articles, the same thought pervades every
discussion. Notes are held to be a part of the
business of banking, to be something more than
cheques drawn by a banker upon himself, which he
is bound to pay on demand, just as he pays the
cheques of his customers. They are regarded as
something radically different from ordinary currency,
from coin, which a banker has to buy and pay for
like his neighbours. They are supposed to form
part of his craft, to be a mystery of which he alone,
and the authorities who have explored its depths,
possess the secret. Whenever any strain presses
upon commerce, and bankers are shy of lending, and
discount mounts swiftly up, and banks tremble for
means wherewith to pay their liabilities, all the
world thinks of banknotes, and either looks for help
from them or lays all the blame of the disaster on
their most innocent heads. No one remembers that
a banker's engagement to his notes is identical with
that which binds him to any cheque from his depositors. When both are laid together on his counter no
human skill can draw any distinction between them.
Whatever differences there may be will be found
solely in the moral probability of the one being
presented rather than the other. Currency will never
be understood by those who persist in mixing it up
with banking ; there will always be an insoluble,

mystical, and unintelligible element in it, so long as
the rate of discount and the state of the money market are associated with it as parts of one organic
whole. Banknotes may easily add to the distress of
a banking pressure, because they may be sent in for
payment at the same time that a flood of cheques
invade the banker from alarmed or impoverished
depositors: and this is a consideration which deserves great attention on the part of the banker and
on the part of those whose duty it is to provide for
the public welfare. But this circumstance does not
alter the nature of a banknote or connect it with a
banker in any other sense than that he is the debtor
who has contracted these debts and must discharge
them. It may be perfectly reasonable for the law to
say that no man shall be allowed to incur so vast a
debt to the public, to an immense aggregate of individuals, all accepting these debts as a matter of
course, almost without any choice in the matter,
unless he gives some security for repayment; but
this does not prove that these debts have a difference for the banker from other debts, except in
the difference in the motives which may lead to
a demand for their settlement. Banknotes must
be studied independently of banks, as sovereigns are
studied independently of the Mint. The Mint is
required to produce a good sovereign; and it is a fit
question to inquire, how a banker shall be made to
produce a sound debt, sure to be paid on demand,
when he puts forth a note into circulation. If a
banker chooses to manufacture these tools of general
demand, the law may call on him for guarantees
for the soundness of these debts, just as it compels
gun-makers to submit to a test of the goodness of

their gun-barrels. So far as a banker is a manufacturer of notes, so far only does banking come into
relation with notes : other institutions besides banks
can issue and have issued notes ; and the questions
thence arising refer exclusively to the goodness of
the manufacturers, and to the quality of the tools
manufactured, and in no way to any organic connection between banking and note issuing.

A banknote, then, is a cheque drawn by a banker
upon himself: ought it to be called money? In
form it exhibits not the slightest difference from any
other cheque : nevertheless it does possess a dis-
tinguishing peculiarity, which raises it to the dignity
and prerogative of money. It circulates; it is current; it performs often an immense number of
exchanges of property before it is sent in for payment and thus ceases to exist. Other cheques are
immediately taken to the bank on which they are
drawn ; a very few occasionally circulate through
two or three persons ; but this is not their function.
Their work is to make one payment and no more ;
the work of the banknote is to make many payments, precisely like coin. The reason of this
difference in the respective careers of the note and
the cheque is plain : the common cheque depends
for its value on the credit which its drawer enjoys,
on the belief that he has money at the bank which
will pay the cheque. In respect of a private person
the worth of this credit is known but to a few. The
man who sells a carriage takes the cheque freely ;
he comes in contact with the drawer, he knows
where he lives, and so on : he is perfectly aware
that it is business not to part with the carriage
before he has ascertained the trustworthiness of

the cheque; and he is willing to take the trouble on himself of discovering this point, because he desires to sell his carriage. When he has got the cheque for 300*l.* he is unable to pass it on to other people as money; they know nothing about the drawer of the cheque, and have no motive for enquiring into his solvency. So the cheque cannot tarry on its road, but finds its way immediately to payment. It is otherwise with the banknote, though its form is the same. The banker and his notes are widely known in his locality. A bank is a kind of public institution. Many persons keep accounts with it; its credit is largely diffused, and the usage naturally establishes itself to take its notes as money. It is not sent in therefore for payment; it remains out in circulation. The question of the banker's solvency in ordinary times occurs to no one, no more than the genuineness of a sovereign, till suspicion is awakened. The old familiar look of the note, like the queen's head on the sovereign, suffices to give it circulation.

And now let us watch the process by which banknotes issue forth into circulation. It is full of instruction on the fundamental points of a paper currency. We all know how an ordinary cheque makes its appearance in the world: goods are bought, a cheque is signed for the cash, and so it commences its short-lived existence. The birth of the banknote takes place in a different manner. It is signed and made ready at the bank; but how does it come forth? Through the payments, few though they be, which the bank makes in cash. It is the office of the banker to lend; and he lends the more freely in proportion as his borrowers carry

away the loans in notes. I am speaking of the first
establishment of its notes in public circulation at
its origin. Observe the fact well; it is the root of
most of the strange delusions afloat in the world
about paper currency. It indissolubly associates in
the commercial mind the issue of notes with perpetual ability to lend. 'The banker,' cries the world,
'most of all the Bank of England, in the hour of
panic, can issue notes which will do the work of
money, and he can lend all the more to traders
accordingly.' And then this fact is insisted on—that
by issuing notes the banker acquires additional
means for lending. The fact is perfectly true ; but
there is an enormous fallacy lurking beneath it. We
shall return to it presently : meanwhile let us go
on with our analysis of the process by which notes
circulate amongst the public.

Such being the manner in which notes commence
their career, the question immediately arises, How
long does it last ? We have learnt that the banknote
possesses the faculty of circulating ; it is impersonal,
so to speak; it comes from a quasi-public authority ;
it can act as money. Still, it may be asked, Why
should it be able to do this? How is it able to
circulate ? To answer that it has the power of
circulation would be merely to beg the question ;
it is no answer. We seek for an explanation of how
it comes to pass, that even though believed to be
safe money, it is not presented for payment in sovereigns, the true coin of the realm, the currency which
carries its own value in its bosom, the precious
wealth which is not, like the paper, a title only
to wealth, but wealth itself. Because, in many
respects, it possesses a very decided superiority

of convenience over gold. It is lighter, and more
easily carried; and this is a merit of the highest
order in currency. Many notes of 1000*l.* each,
move about the city; 60,000*l.* or 80,000*l.* not unfrequently are borne in pockets or portfolios, from
house to house; conceive the embarrassment, the
weight, the reckoning, the trouble and risk of carrying away so many thousand sovereigns. Then,
the banknote can be more easily protected against
robbery; it is handier to stow away; and the
number which it bears facilitates detection and
enables its payment to be stopped at the bank.
It will not be so efficient amongst strangers as
in the bank's locality at home. So strong is this
principle of local attachment, that in Scotland, and
even in parts of England, the notes of local bankers
are preferred to those of the Bank of England.
Where it is known and respected the banknote tri-
umphantly asserts its superiority over the sovereign.
So fond are the Scotch people of this money that it
is often easier to get change for a banknote than
for a sovereign in Scotland—a striking illustration
of the sagacity and intelligence of Scotchmen.

And now we reach the most important question
of all—In what numbers will these banknotes circulate? It is the crucial question wherewith to test
the soundness of every theory of currency. It is a
question which every merchant, every banker, every
chamber of commerce, every member of Parliament
who speaks on currency, ought to push home to his
mind, and not be content till he has attained to a
clear, precise, and intelligible answer. It is the
centre of every theory of currency whether metallic
or of paper. Every doctrine which is mistaken on

this central principle is worthless as an interpreter
of the science of currency. Mr. Tooke discerned the
true answer: Mr. Mill, with some little wavering,
and a few others, have seen the light; but the
general literature on money matters throughout the
world profoundly ignores the fact. The answer is
the same with that which has already been given
to the parallel question respecting sovereigns. So
many banknotes as the public wants and can use
will circulate and no more. Neither the bankers,
nor Parliament, nor the law, nor the need of borrowers, nor any other power, but the wants and
convenience of the public, the number and amount
of the specific payments in which banknotes are
used, can determine how many convertible banknotes will remain in circulation and not be returned
upon the hands of the bankers for payment. This
is the truth of truths in currency. The banker may
have the strongest inclination to issue more; eager
merchants, in their anxiety to procure loans, may
offer to carry away in notes the whole of their
borrowings; Chancellors of the Exchequer may
grant suspensions of Acts of Parliament to fathers
of the City; but the attempt to substitute any other
regulator of the quantity of the notes circulating
than the inclination of the public to keep them is
absolutely hopeless. An expanded or inflated circulation of banknotes is an absurdity, nothing better
than pure nonsense. It would be just as sensible
to speak of an expanded or inflated circulation of
hats. It is easy enough for the hatter to make more
hats than can be sold; but where is the inflation
in that case? In the number of hats circulating
about the town, in each man having a dozen hats

in his house? The very question is puerile. There would be an inflation of hats, but it would be found in the shops of the hatters, and not in the circulation of hats. There may be in the same way an inflation of banknotes by too many being made; but the inflation would not be found in the circulation of notes, but in the banks, which would be stuffed up with their own unuseable and unsaleable wares. Ask each of yourselves, how it is possible to inflate your own use of banknotes? The question itself excites your ridicule. What is to make you willing to keep more banknotes in your desks or your pockets, so long as your habits of spending remain unchanged and you have enough for your regular wants? If more should reach you from any source, what would you do with them? Keep them? No; you would get rid of them: you would place them at a banker's, as things for which you have no specific use, so long as your habits of life remain unaltered. I mean by habits of life, not your spending more, but your spending in a way which creates a new use for notes. A gift of 100*l.* in notes might send you on a travel—and then you would want more notes; but your spending them at Oxford in buying furniture or books would not increase your want of notes. You would put the notes at a bank, and pay for the furniture and books with cheques. The same inability to increase the use of notes, and the consequent unwillingness to retain them which you experience, beset every member of the community. All except the lowest classes do not in England receive or spend their incomes in money. If a duke wishes to go to Edinburgh, he must bring either a banknote or some sovereigns to the station, or he

will get no ticket : but he may spend an income of
100,000*l.* a-year and scarcely ever touch money.
The truth is suffocated by abstractions. The commercial world pants for more notes. 'Give us notes,'
cry the borrowers ; 'we know that we want them
and can use them. We can pay our debts, and
meet our engagements with them, and is not that
a real and capital use for notes ?' 'Away with the
Bank Charter Act,' exclaim these passionate traders :
'the Bank of England possesses instruments which
cost it nothing, but which every seller in the shops
will take, which will satisfy every importunate creditor, and give us access to every warehouse. Suffer
the Bank to open its stores without restriction,
and to place in our hands the saviours of our fortunes.' Such is the vehement feeling of merchants
frantic at the approach of ruin ; and grave writers,
men of wealth and weight, and ministers of State,
and even Parliament, countenance the delusion. They
invent all kinds of doctrines to support this sure
specific for easy borrowing and easy lending. That
the expansion of the nation's wealth requires an
enlarged currency of banknotes, is laid down as a
fundamental principle of science by an elaborate
circular of a chamber of commerce. 'To restrict
the supply of banknotes is to stifle commerce. A
contracted circulation raises prices. A limitation
on the issue of notes raises the rate of interest
charged by bankers on discounting merchants' bills.'
But where do these gentlemen get all these fine
principles ? Not from scientific analysis of facts :
they must be primitive truths seized by the mercantile mind by intuition, self-evident axioms requiring no other evidence than their own light to

establish them. But again, I ask, how can the
public be induced to retain the notes in circulation?
Everything turns on this question; yet it is the
very question which these authorities always choose
to ignore. No one faces it; no one puts it; no one
asks what is the motive, what is the influence which
determines the public to use notes, be they fewer,
more, or the same to-day as yesterday. That the cry
for loans and discount is very sharp is argument
enough for the City that more notes are wanted:
there it stops. The Bank, they say, if the Act of
1844 were repealed, could lend the notes with perfect
ease; the borrowers are only too eager to get them.
But what if the notes are brought back to the
Bank for payment an hour or two later? The borrower to whom the notes have been given so freely
at once transfers them to his creditor: what the
creditor does with them becomes the vital question.
Does he want them as notes, as money? By no
means, for the loan of fresh notes by the Bank to
his debtor created no new use of notes for him. He
will not keep more notes in his pocket, or employ
more in his business, because notes have been issued
to some other person. No doubt he required to
have his debt paid, but he did not require payment
in money for keeping; and if he receives money he
carries it at once to his banker. No one keeps more
money at home than he can use. Neither does the
banker want the notes, for his business lies with
cheques and bills; and since the case we are supposing of a forced issue of extra notes implies that
the public, including the banker, had already enough
for their wants, these notes are as redundant to the
banker as they were to the creditor who received

I

them from the man who borrowed them of the issuing bank. So the banker sends them on to the issuing bank for payment. Not a single person among the public has had his want and use of notes increased by the loan granted by the issuing banker; not a single additional motive for retaining them has been created. Like the supernumerary sovereigns, they must be stored away as lumber; that is, they must flow back to the source from which they sprang, and be extinguished.

And now consider the position of the issuing banker. The common notion ascribes to him the power of issuing notes at pleasure; but he finds in practice that he lies under the most rigorous restriction. Every note he put forth was a debt which he was contracting, a debt subject to the formidable condition of being instantly paid on demand under pain of bankruptcy. He issued the notes because the borrower was urgent, and perhaps public opinion pressed him, as it often presses the Bank of England; a few hours later he is called upon to pay those very notes himself out of his own resources. With his other notes, the notes required and kept in circulation by the ordinary business of the country, he acquired means from the public, who paid him for the notes; the public bought them for use, for consumption, so to say, and does not send them back for payment. What the public gave for these notes were additional resources placed in the hands of the banker; and as the notes remain in circulation, the banker can lend out these new resources without danger. But from these additional notes lent to a borrower after the wants of the public are fully supplied, the banker gets no new re-

sources at all ; they are lent to merchants without
being paid for ; and then, when they are presented
a few hours later, the banker is actually obliged to
pay them out of his own means. What, then, does
all this rotation amount to ? To this hard and
inevitable fact — that when a banker lends such
extra notes to a borrower, he is in fact not lending
notes at all, but making a loan out of his own
resources, which is given a little later, when the
notes are presented for payment. These extra notes
furnish no additional faculty of making advances
to traders, because the public will not keep them,
but will insist on their being paid out of the banker's
means. His resources are augmented by issuing
notes precisely to the extent to which the public
wants notes for daily use, in making those payments
in which notes actually pass with a certain stock
in reserve, and to not a single pound more. The
cry for more notes is senseless, and impossible to
gratify. Neither bankers nor Parliament can prevent convertible notes that are not wanted from
being extinguished by a demand on the general means
of the issuer.

Fact confirms this view. The Bank of England,
before 1844, had a completely unrestricted liberty
of issuing notes at its own sole discretion ; the law
in no way interfered with its freedom. Well, under
this uncontrolled latitude, the Bank found itself as
much restricted in the issue of notes as it is now
alleged to be by statute. The restriction lay in
the very essence of every currency, in the limitation
of the power of consuming, which is attached to
every commodity under the sun. The banknotes
were limited down and curtailed by the spontaneous

action of the public; and the Bank in those days could not and did not make larger advances with notes than she does now. The only difference between the two periods is this—that before 1844, whatever gold was taken into the Bank, was simply put into store, generally without a single note being issued against it; since 1844, notes are given at the State's office of the issue department in exchange for all gold received: but these notes do not circulate, they clog the till of the banking department. In fact, they serve merely as receipts.

Next comes the same question which met us in a metallic currency, and it will necessarily receive the same answer. What does the public want notes for? What is the sort of employment they are put to, so that one may be able to understand when a paper currency is full? A currency is full, I reply, when there are notes enough for cashiers of banks, as they receive and pay the three pounds of cash out of the hundred which constitute the business of banks; when those who wish to carry notes about can procure the number they require; when frightened bankers, with means in hand, can attain a sufficient supply for hoarding in their reserves; when no trade, no sale, is stopped by a deficiency of note-change. Notes are seldom the currency in which advances or loans are made: most advances are given by a line placed in a ledger to the credit of the borrower, who then draws out by degrees this power of buying and paying. In Scotland, which is fond of paper currency and cleaves to one pound notes, the quantity which I have termed 'enough' will be, relatively to the amount of business going on in the country, much larger than in Eng-

land; because notes are there used in those small
payments which in England are effected by sovereigns. They reach the small retail business all
over the land; they have more work to do, and
must therefore muster in greater numbers. But in
England, in Scotland, and in all cases and countries
alike, the universal principle stands paramount, the
fact remains dominant, that notes are needed merely
to act as money in those transactions in which,
according to the habits of the country, money is
actually employed,—that they are tools for a specific
work, as knives are for cutting, and carts for drawing,—that the question about them is always the
same as for every other article sold in shops, namely,
whether there is enough of them for the particular
office they have to perform, and never whether there
is enough to make loans and advances with in times
of commercial difficulty and pressure. For 97 parts
out of 100 of the transfers of property, made in
actual life, money is not used at all. Money has
no other object than to transfer the ownership of
property; and it performs only three per cent. of the
whole of the work which has to be done. When
once the mind has succeeded in forming the habit
of always thinking of the note as an instrument
for certain special payments, currency will have
become intelligible and natural, for the elements
of perplexity will have been swept away. On the
other hand, if the use of banknotes is connected
with the ups and downs of trade, in such a manner
that their regulation by the law or by the bankers
is supposed to facilitate loans, and to act upon the
rate of discount, and to avert panics, and to save
commerce, currency must continue to be the one

inscrutable mystery amongst the sciences. The infusion of heterogeneous and arbitrary elements into any department of knowledge is destructive of all science. Theorists retarded astronomy, when they insisted that the planets must move in circles, because the Creator would not allow them to rotate in imperfect curves; and theorists equally render currency unintelligible, when they preach that currency is a regulator instead of being a humble instrument of trade.

The preceding explanation, you will observe, implies that the demand for banknotes varies immensely at different times. It is no new phenomenon for us; we have met with it already in a metallic currency. The fluctuations in the number of notes in circulation are much greater yet than those of gold, at least in England; at times, they are largely hoarded by bankers and merchants. It has been urged against my view of currency, that I ignore the vast demand which occasionally springs up for banknotes, as was seen in the memorable crisis of 1866. I am thus accused of treating the supply of banknotes as a matter of trifling significance. Those who bring this charge against me cannot have been at the pains of understanding what I say; it would be as rational to accuse me of ignoring the variations in the demand for blankets because I call a blanket an instrument for keeping one's-self warm in bed. I have never denied the desirableness of having a full supply of banknotes; but, undoubtedly, I have not attributed the same importance to a deficiency as my opponents. But of this more presently. As to variations in the demand for notes, my answer is, that I have pointed them out on all fitting occasions. The use of notes must vary, according as the number of payments which the public makes with banknotes varies. My main principle, that a note is a tool for a definite specific work, which itself itself varies, implies a variation in the use of the note. When business is active, and increased buying is going on at the shops, and more salaries are given, and larger hosts of travellers throng the trains, the demand for banknotes necessarily rises. Still greater yet is the eagerness to get possession of them when panic has seized on commerce. At such times, men are disposed to distrust the strongest and best-managed banks; they like to keep their money in their own custody at home. Merchants, whose bills must be met on pain of ruin, prefer to have the money under their own eyes, rather than entrust it to even the Bank of England, lest it might be lent to borrowers, and not be forthcoming for their own wants. Most of all the countless banks in England arm themselves at such seasons with additional notes; they draw deeper on the Bank of England for them in various ways, and a larger issue must come forth. On the other hand, when confidence revives, or trade grows slacker, the now unneeded notes flow back to the bank. The public cannot hold them; it has a diminished use for such tools, they must retire under cover as a farmer's ploughs at harvest-time. Hence the interest which I attach to the weekly returns of the circulation of the Bank of England is one of statistics only. They indicate certain movements in trade to and fro; but they reveal nothing as to their nature, and can have no influence in controlling them. The creation of a dozen new clearing-houses in the great towns would seriously diminish

the use of banknotes. A clearing-house at the west
end of London would sensibly reduce the circulation
of banknotes: instead of keeping notes to pay over
the counter, the west-end bankers would settle their
respective demands on each other without employing
a single note. Yet, would any change have been
produced upon trade by the institution of such
a clearing-house? Would the diminished figures of
the circulation indicate anything more than the
establishing of new clearing-houses, and the substitution of one mode of payment for another? There
would be the same quantity of business, the same
amount of payments, the same number of cheques,
but an amazing reduction in the circulation of banknotes. Writers on currency never condescend to
study this obvious and certain fact; they shrink
from the inference which it irresistibly compels. The
stress they lay on the amount of the circulation,
the significance they attach to its numbers, the connection which they establish between these numbers
and the prosperity or adversity of trade, could not
live by the side of such a fact, as that the springing
up of clearing-houses would vastly affect the amount
of the circulation. The weekly returns of the circulation, which you see published in the 'Times,' tell
nothing more about the state of trade than would
returns of the business done in a grocer's shop;
nay, not nearly so much; for the fluctuations in
the buying at the grocer's are fluctuations of actual
wealth, whilst the fluctuations of banknotes are
variations of an instrument of exchange only. They
testify to the habits of the moment only; to the
chance employment of one set of tools rather than
another, and to nothing else.

There is, however, an ignorance which lies at the root of all these illusions—the ignorance of the true nature of a bank's means and the source from which they spring. If the analysis which I have given you of the real character of a bank's operations had been made and understood, banknotes would never have acquired this exaggerated importance. The City believes that it holds in its hands, within its own walls, the vast wealth which the countless figures in so many ledgers indicate. No mistake can be more thorough or more radical. A great City bank, say the London and Westminster, is described as possessing twenty millions sterling of deposits: the imagination lays hold of this huge sum as being so much money; and the current of thought and language is governed by the impression thus received. But where, I ask, is all this wealth? In the London and Westminster Bank? In what part of its splendid buildings? In its till? Look and see; you will not find the sovereigns and banknotes of the huge total there. In its cellars? Not there, either. Where is it, then? In actual existence, as wealth, it is not in the London and Westminster Bank at all. Twenty millions of deposits mean that the bank owes twenty millions of money; and if the bank is sound, the turning over the pages of the ledger will show that other people owe the bank as much. The ledger, and, barring the small cash in hand, the mere change lying in its till, the ledger alone is the bank. The City is but one great accountant's office. Its merchants, its bankers—all who do not possess actual merchandize within its boundaries—are only clerks employed in the distribution of wealth. They are clerks who give orders, no doubt; but the buying

to sell again without touching the goods, the letters,
the moneys, the account sales, the balancing of accounts by debtor and creditor, the setting off of
debts, the settlement by cheques and bills, are all
nothing but machinery—machinery for the most part
made of paper. The wealth and capital of England
are not in merchants' offices or bankers' ledgers; not
in bills and balances; they are spread over the
whole land: they are England itself, and all that
it contains. If the City could thoroughly grasp
this great truth, it would not fall so lightly into
the delusion that a bank with the power of issuing
notes has unlimited stores to lend. Wealth and
capital are not the things which a bank lends, for
a bank does not possess them: it possesses only the
power to procure them. A bank receives bills and
cheques, and lends out bills and cheques; but bills
and cheques are not wealth, though they are very
efficient in procuring wealth. Neither is a banknote
wealth: it is a piece of paper, nothing more. It has
important and very effective words written upon it;
but those written words are not more effective than
spoken ones, when the speaker is known and trusted.
Banknotes do not procure goods more effectively
than the orders given at shops, registered in the colossal book debts throughout the nation. A banknote
is a title, an evidence, a proof, which will lead to the
acquisition of coin or goods; but so also a few
words uttered by a known person in a shop will
equally end in the acquisition of goods. A banker
obtains from his customers purchasing power—power
to buy wealth, and this is what he distributes to
others: that power is contained in debts, in claims
owned by his clients, which they have transferred to

him; and he passes it on to borrowers. It is the same with his note. A banknote is a contrivance by which a banker obtains from the public a purchasing power which he transfers to others with a profit for himself. The banker, by the act of issuing, first becomes a borrower; he incurs a debt himself. Lend me, he says to the public, the means of obtaining five pounds' worth of the goods sold in shops and warehouses, and I will undertake to give you five sovereigns when you ask for them. The public consents, grants him the loan, and takes his receipt in the form of his banknote. But why is the public willing to lend to him, or, to alter the form of the expression, why is the public willing to buy his note? In other words, how is it that a permanent circulation of banknotes exists? Because the public, for carrying out its buyings and sellings, must buy either five sovereigns or a banknote, and prefers the note. That is the one simple and decisive answer. That is the reason why the public consents to grant a loan to the banker and accepts and retains his note. For certain operations of buying and selling—few though they be in respect of the totality—the public must have sovereigns or notes; and, according to the statement of Sir John Lubbock, prefers the notes in the proportion of five to one. This mode of statement renders the true nature of the fact apparent. It is the public, and in no way the banker, who is the real agent in the matter, whose will regulates and controls the issues, who decides whether the banker shall be allowed to borrow and contract a debt with notes, and to what extent this borrowing shall be permitted.

This fact, that notes in circulation are loans made

by the public to the bank, or, which means the same thing, are useful tools purchased by the public from the bank, disposes of the common idea that bankers and traders together can settle how many notes shall be issued, and how much accommodation, as it is called, shall be given. It is the lender and not the borrower who has the decision in lending : it is the customer and not the shopkeeper who settles how many guns or umbrellas shall be in use : it is the public, and not the banker and trader together, which determines how many notes it will use, and at what point of the circulation it will send in every additional note for payment. The Bank of England in times of crisis may have the best disposition in the world to lend by issuing notes ; merchants may raise imploring cries at her doors ; they may bring their warrants of merchandize in the docks, their stocks and their shares, their mortgages and their silver as guarantees and securities for repayment—it will all be to no purpose. The bank may issue notes ; but the public will not buy them because its want for notes is supplied, and back the notes come in an hour or two, and, if there is to be lending, it must be the bank and not the public that shall be the lender. The bank will have to lend out of its own resources, and not out of means supplied to it by the public. The capacity of the public to use notes, and not the willingness of borrowers to take them out from the bank, is the power which alone determines how many notes shall be issued.

The preceding explanation will have shown you, that in preferring a banknote to a sovereign for doing the same identical work, the public has earned a great saving ; for a sovereign costs twenty shillings'

worth of England's property to buy, and the piece
of paper has not cost a farthing. The one identical
service can be performed by either alike, and no
one has any interest in choosing a more expensive
material for making a tool when a cheaper and
equally efficient one may be obtained. No one rigs
a vessel with silken cordage. There is a saving,
then, of twenty shillings : who gets it ? The capital
of the country is practically augmented by the substitution of a paper for a metallic currency. Who
reaps the benefit of this capital ? The wealth which
would have bought the gold remains in England :
whom does this saving belong to ? The nation,
collectively, no doubt : yet practically it is not the
general public which receives the profit and acquires
the use of this saving. The whole of this wealth
falls to the enjoyment of the bankers who issue
notes. The public pays for its currency the same
actual price in either case : it has to buy with
twenty shillings' worth of goods a sovereign from
a gold-miner or a banknote from a banker. None
of us gain anything by our purchases being made by
one of these instruments rather than the other. The
persons who employ currency are unaffected by the
change ; but the issuing bankers are largely benefited.
They obtain from the public the amount of property
reckoned up in the banknotes, and they lend it out
to borrowers with a profit to themselves. Nevertheless the nation also reaps a second and indirect
benefit. The stock of capital is substantially increased by the portion which would have been sent
to foreign miners for the purchase of gold or silver.
England is so much the richer for the change ; and
an increase of capital is a benefit to the whole people,

whoever may be the individuals who derive most advantage from it. There are increased means for employing and remunerating labour; there is more to lend, and the charge for lending it may be reduced.

But now arises a question of vast importance. Banknotes are debts contracted by a banker. The public has lent him money, or the equivalent of money, for them. He is answerable for repayment. What guarantee does the public possess, or ought to possess, that these notes will be repaid on demand? The notes penetrate all over society; they are taken as trustworthy pledges of value in exchange for every kind of property; they are treated as thoroughly safe debts, of sure and certain solvency, and fit, therefore, to pass from hand to hand, and to be taken by every seller as a perfect security that he shall be able to purchase with them other goods of the same value as those that he has sold. The discovery that these debts were worthless, the failure to pay the money due upon them on demand, would strip the holders of them of the property they believed that they possessed, and would spread disaster over the whole land. What security is there, or ought to be, against the occurrence of such a calamity? The sovereign can claim the transcendent merit of carrying its own security within itself. If the sovereign is a good one, there can be no loss in giving merchandize in exchange for it. But the same assurance can never be felt about the payment of any debt—even were it a debt due by a great people like England. The bond can never be as absolutely safe as the metal itself. Nevertheless, though this is so, debts are universally

contracted among all civilized nations without difficulty; and the bankers' debts find buyers, though
by no means always sure to be paid when demanded.
On what, then, do the holders of banknotes, these
purchasers of a banker's debts, these voluntary lenders
of their property to bankers, rely? What induces
them not to demand the gold specified upon a note, in
the same way as they require the money ordered in
a cheque? Up to 1844, the only security which
those who took banknotes possessed was the property of the banker. His reputation for wealth, for
integrity, for skill and judgment in the management
of his business, in one word, his credit, alone gave
circulation to his notes. No one was compelled to
accept them, whether on the sale of goods or in
discharge of liabilities; they were voluntarily taken
on trust; they circulated about town and country,
from a common feeling that so respectable a person
as the banker would be certain to meet his engagements. Hence the law treated the liability of the
banker for his notes as a common debt, with the
provision that a refusal to pay the note constituted
an act of bankruptcy. The assets of the bank and
the property of the banker were the only guarantees
for payment and convertibility; and to this day
a large amount of notes in the United Kingdom rests
on no other foundation. This system has worked
most successfully in Scotland, as also with the Bank
of England note; but elsewhere it has been attended
with frequent and overwhelming disasters. 'The
destruction of country banks in England,' says Mr.
MacCulloch, 'has upon three different occasions, in
1792, in 1814, 1815, and 1816, and in 1825 and
1826, produced an extent of bankruptcy and misery

that has never, perhaps, been equalled, except by
the breaking-up of the Mississippi scheme in France.
In 1826, forty-three commissions of bankruptcy were
issued against country bankers; and from 1809 to
1830 no less than 311. During the whole of this
period not a single Scotch bank gave way.'

The simple guarantee of the bank's assets was
thus perfectly successful in Scotland, and very calamitous in England: holders of Scotch notes lost
nothing, holders of English notes were again and
again ruined. But I pray you to observe that the
difference between the two results in no way proceeded from any variation in the systems of currency
adopted in the two countries. The method of issuing
notes and providing for their convertibility was
identical in both. The failure in the one case and
the success in the other were exclusively events of
banking, in no degree events of currency. The
causes which made the Scotch tills full and the
English tills empty had their existence entirely
within the banking trade. The Scotch issuers of
notes were good bankers and kept their money, the
English were bad bankers and lost it: so the creditors of the first were paid in full, and the creditors
of the latter, note-holders and ordinary customers
alike, sometimes got no more than half-a-crown in
the pound.

These public calamities raised the inquiry, whether
the duty was not incumbent on the State to provide
protection by law against their recurrence. The
interference of the Legislature was demanded by
public opinion; and it becomes very necessary to
arrive at a clear understanding of the principle on
which such a demand can be sustained.

LECTURE V.

THE BANK CHARTER ACT OF 1844, AND MR. MILL'S DOCTRINE OF MONEY.

OUR first task to-day is to answer the question with which the last lecture terminated: What is the principle on which the special interference of the law with the particular kind of cheque called a banknote is claimed and justified? Up to the year 1844, the payment of the banknote rested simply on the general law of debt; but the disastrous losses suffered by the holders of country notes in 1825, and at other periods, created a conviction in the public mind that some action of the law for the protection of society was needed in this matter. Yet why should one form of debt demand special legislation beyond all others? Cheques are frequently not paid: the non-payment of bills is constantly bringing loss and ruin on innocent persons: yet the law is not found to be stepping forward with enactments which render the non-payment of a cheque or a bill almost impossible. A banknote is but a cheque: whence the distinction in his case compared with the failures of

K

his brethren ? They are left to take their chance.
The State considers them as matters belonging
to purely private management, in which it feels
no other responsibility than the general enforce-
ment of the payment of all debts and of the fulfilment of all contracts. The mere fact that one class
of debts is liable to frequent non-payment does not,
of itself alone, constitute a claim for exceptional legislation. Some distinctive feature in their nature must
be shown before a basis for special enactments of law
can be obtained. The question, then, is, Does the
banknote present any such peculiarity of nature ?
Is there anything in the character and functions of
a banknote which calls on the State to issue exceptional ordinances for its regulation ?

The public has judged that such a demand for
legislative interference exists, and has judged rightly.
Writers of great ability and distinction, such, for
instance, as M. Michel Chevalier, have repelled such
interference as a violation of the great principle that
the liberty of trade should not be controlled by the
State. They have insisted on the right of a banker
to issue his notes, his obligations to pay, without
control, if the public is willing to purchase them.
Freedom to issue these particular cheques is demanded as a right inherent in the business of banking, as absolutely as the right of a merchant to
purchase a cargo of silk with a bill. The right,
therefore, of a banker to put forth his notes without
any interference from the law is made to rest on
the general principle that every trader is entitled
to conduct his business in any way that he chooses.
But is there any such universal principle capable
of claiming such unlimited authority ? Is it true,

in reason or in fact, that the management of a trade can never be regulated by law without a breach of freedom and of natural right? Are no limitations ever set on the acts of traders with the sanction and approbation of public opinion? What shall we say of the laws which prescribe minute regulations for the control of passenger vessels? Is every cabman allowed to ply in the streets without any check on his movements or his fares? May a manufacturer of gunpowder or glycerine transport his goods about the world at his pleasure under no restriction from authority? Can a gunmaker sell guns which have not been proved by a public official? In all these cases the law interferes, and prescribes and limits, and society approves the interference, and no cries about tyrannical restrictions are heard from traders. The interference is justified on the perfectly sufficient ground, that it is called for by the safety and the welfare of the whole community. The individual efforts of each private person for himself are insufficient to procure the safety which is indispensable for him and the rest of the world. The State must be summoned to do what it alone can perform.

No principle, then, of unlimited liberty to trade can be invoked which forbids in all cases the intervention of the Government: let us see whether any reasons can be found which show that the business of issuing banknotes is one which requires a special action of the law. Why should security be taken by the law for the payment of a banknote, whilst the solvency of a cheque or of a bill is allowed to remain unprotected? Can reasons be assigned for such exceptional interference? Good and solid reasons, I answer, can be alleged, and they will be

found in the vastness of the public interest involved
in the issue of banknotes, and in the peculiarity of
their nature. You need consider only for a moment
the immensity of the calamity if the twenty or thirty
millions of Bank of England notes were suddenly to
become worthless, in order to be convinced of the
strong public importance of effectually guarding
against the occurrence of such a disaster. If it were
practically possible, if such wide-spread ruin and
misery could be conceived as events which, however
improbable, might actually come to pass, no thoughtful man would hesitate an instant in concluding that
no people ought ever to be exposed to such a danger,
and that the advantages of a paper currency were
light as a feather in the scale when weighed against
such a misfortune. A thousand times better would
it be to discard paper money altogether, and to employ exclusively money made of metal. The magnitude to which the issues of a particular bank may be
developed greatly aggravates the peril, as it would
multiply the ruin. The difference is enormous between
a circulation of half a million and one of twenty-five
millions. In the absence of any other regulation,
the restriction of the circulation of any single bank's
issues to a million would prevent the failure of
any bank from rising to the significance of a national
calamity.

But secondly, a marked practical distinction exists
between the mode of circulation of a common cheque
and that of a banknote. The cheque emanates from
a private person. Its value depends on his means,
or rather on the presence of those means at the
bank when his cheque is presented for payment.
The affairs of private persons are unknown to the

general public; the worth of their cheques must therefore be necessarily obscure for the world at large. By their very nature they are unfit to circulate, to be used as money, and to be kept by the public as instruments of exchange. All these considerations are more or less present to the minds of those who take cheques in payment. Every one knows that he is bound to consider whether the cheque is a good one and is sure to be paid; everyone is aware that in parting with his goods for a cheque, the duty lies on him to assure himself on this vital point; and every one also knows that a cheque ought to be sent in immediately for payment. No special action of the law is needed for cheques; because the action of each individual man affords sufficient security for the safe employment of cheques. It is otherwise with the banknote. A bank is a kind of public institution. Its business is widely known, and interests a large number of persons. It is thus invested with a public character. Its notes become something more than the cheques of a private person. Even though they are voluntarily taken, and may be sent in for payment at any hour, they remain in circulation, and pass from hand to hand, and in every respect, by common consent, assume the nature and attributes of money. Thus the taking of them in payment is not so purely a voluntary act as the taking of a cheque. There is a kind of semi-compulsion pressing on the man to whom they are offered. The tradesman who rejected them would run the risk of losing his customer, who might be tempted into the rival shop, where no objection would be made to his money; offence might be given to the numerous friends and

customers of the bank throughout the town. No
doubt there is always the remedy of demanding gold
for them; but the habit of the world is against that
process. A shopkeeper cannot be at that trouble
every day; he finds that he can pass the notes as
easily as he took them, and that is enough for him.
Unless some remarkable event has drawn attention
to the affairs of the bank, no one thinks of the
solvency of the notes; they find their way into every
purse as a matter of course. It is impossible not to
discover in these facts a manifest weakness of the
public to protect itself adequately against the non-
payment of the banknote. Doubtless it might do
much more in that direction if it chose; but, as
a matter of fact, it does not; and when the day
of failure arrives, a large portion of the common-
wealth finds itself involved in loss, often of a very
disastrous kind. This is the ground on which the
interference of the law is justified and demanded.
A public danger is thus disclosed, against which
individual action furnishes no adequate guarantee;
and, just as the State provides for the general safety
in respect of guns and powder and emigrant ships,
so it can and it ought to provide sufficient security
for the goodness of the public money.

The question now arises, what ought these
guarantees to be? Three have been adopted, and
are now actually at work. The first consists in the
good management and banking skill of the issuing
bank. This is not a guarantee created by law, and
consequently does not carry out the principle of
a security devised and enforced by statute. I do
not say, then, that theoretically it is the fitting
guarantee, or that it can be relied upon for safety

at all times and under all circumstances. Nevertheless, when it does exist, where there are that actual banking skill and good management, they do the required work as efficiently as a security defined and prescribed by law. Up to 1844 it was the only security possessed by the public for the largest circulation in the world; and to this hour it constitutes the guarantee for most Scotch and English country notes, as well as for the issues of the Bank of France and other foreign institutions. It has worked with perfect success in the cases of the Bank of England and of the Scotch notes. I believe that not a single person ever suffered loss in Scotland from the non-payment of banknotes; and we know this to be true of the Bank of England at all times when its notes were convertible and not forbidden to be paid in gold. There never has existed any practical motive, much less any practical necessity, which called for a change in the systems of Scotland and of the Bank of England. The Bank of England note, since the Bank Restriction Act was repealed and payment on demand enforced by law, has enjoyed the most untainted reputation for solvency and credit. The Act of 1844 has not rendered the Bank of England note one whit better, or sounder, or more deserving of circulation, than it was before that period. It is very desirable to note this fact well. The Act of 1844 added only a theoretical security to the issues of the Bank of England. Practically, and as a matter of fact—and matter of fact is the only thing of importance here — the Bank of England note was as good before 1844 as it is now. The law of that year was not called for by the faintest suspicion resting on the solidity of the

Bank of England note; and, therefore, when you hear persons praising that Act for having made that note safe, you will do well to remember that the safety bestowed by it was the safety conferred by an extra door and an extra lock on a building already impenetrable to robbers. I do not find fault with this additional security; only I cannot admit, that in the case of this particular bank, or in that of the Scotch notes, it had any practical value. The desire to make the Bank of England note safe, and to guarantee its convertibility, was not in any degree the motive which influenced its authors to promote the enactment of that measure. That motive is often assigned now; but it is an after-thought. Their real aim was to act on the circulation; to provide machinery which should contract the amount of banknotes according as gold ebbed away from the Bank. The Act was designed as a remedy against drains: an absurd and impracticable scheme. The fact that the ancient credit in public estimation of the old Bank of England note before 1844 equalled its present repute, was emphatically asserted by Alderman Salomons before a Committee of the House of Commons; and the assertion was strictly correct. So far, then, the public gained nothing by the Bank Charter Act; but the matter is quite otherwise with the notes of country banks throughout England. These banks had failed by hundreds. Their method of banking was unsound and disastrous. They were bad bankers, and often lost their means; and then those who held their notes were involved in ruinous losses. Public opinion recognized that the paper money issued by these banks did not fulfil the indispensable condition of solvency, and that a remedy

ought to be imperiously demanded from the law.
Bankers who conducted their business ill were manifestly unfit persons to be entrusted with the function
of supplying public money. They were bad makers,
bad manufacturers, unfit to be trusted with the
work; as bad as a mint whose sovereigns could never
be relied upon for quality. The remedy came in
1844; and, whatever else may be said of the Act then
passed, it is certain that, so long as it remains in
force, the special disasters of 1825 can never recur.

A second mode of securing the convertibility and
payment of the banknote is that adopted for the
Bank of England by the Act of 1844. That statute
erected a self-acting piece of machinery, which vir-
tually took away from the Bank of England the
issue of those notes which still bear its name. The
Directors of the Bank of England no longer issue
notes. The Bank of England has become a non-
issuing bank. Its Directors have nothing whatever
to do with the Bank of England notes. The Act of
1844 has lodged the power of issuing notes in a
special organ or institution which has been most
inaccurately and most unfortunately styled 'The
Issue Department of the Bank of England.' It is
not a department of the Bank in any sense. It is
a self-acting institution of the State, working on the
Bank's premises, and directed by rules laid down by
the State, and absolutely beyond the control of the
Bank Directors. In their own room, in the parlour
of what is called their own Department of Issue,
the Directors have no more power or influence than
any other man in the country who has a Bank of
England note in his hand. This Government office
issues the notes. First of all, it puts fifteen millions

in the hands of the Bank of England without asking
for a pound of coin in return. The Government owes
fourteen millions to the Bank. I do not say that these
fourteen millions are pledged to the holders of these
fifteen millions of notes, for the point has never been
legally decided ; but anyhow, it is undisputed that the
Bank is a creditor of the Government for fourteen millions, that it receives no interest on this debt, and consequently that the use of the fifteen millions of notes
without payment may be regarded as the means for
compensating the Bank for this loss of interest and
for the expense of managing the National Debt.
Well, then, the Automaton has issued fifteen millions
of notes, and given them over for use to the Bank
of England ; but that is not enough for circulation.
The public wants a larger quantity of notes for use ;
and the Automaton accordingly has its machinery
so arranged as to give the public with one hand any
number of notes beyond the fifteen millions that it
chooses to ask for, and with the other to collect from
the same public as much gold as these notes come to.
This gold is deposited downstairs in the cellar. By
this arrangement the convertibility of the Bank's notes
beyond fifteen millions is placed completely out of jeo-
pardy ; for there are five sovereigns in the vaults for
every note issued beyond that figure. The first fifteen
millions are either made safe by the debt due by the
Government of fourteen millions, if the courts of law
should rule that the debt constitutes a specific security
for these notes ; or else they are included amongst
the collective debts of the Bank, for which all the
property of the Bank, this great Government debt
included, is liable. It is obvious that the effect of
this statute, so far as the Bank of England is con-

cerned, is to make the circulation practically metallic
with the exception of fifteen millions; and as the
working of the Act is sure to extinguish, in process
of time, the notes now issued by country bankers,
substituting in their place the notes of the Bank of
England, the ultimate result will be, that the whole
currency of England—all its money, both coin and
paper, beyond the fifteen millions lent to the Bank
—will be metallic. And now what judgment must
be passed upon the character of these regulations
upon the principles of pure currency alone, without
any reference to the rate of discount or the Money
Market, or any consideration connected with
banking? First of all, it is clear that the banknote, supposing the country circulation to have
been extinguished, is placed on the highest level
of safety and stability. This is the capital point,
undoubtedly : that is, an unsafe note, a note not
likely to be paid on demand, is a form of money in
the highest degree vicious and illegitimate. The
goodness of money, the purity of the metal and the
soundness of the debt acknowledged by the note,
is the one quality which enables it to discharge its
function well, and ought always to be regarded as
indispensable. But, it may be asked, is the retaining
of the gold in the cellar the natural and most fitting
method of securing the good quality of a banknote ?
That the presence of the gold at hand renders the
note safe is incontestable ; but the question is this :
is the having the gold in hand the sole, the necessary,
the one paramount condition of safety ? The re-
tention in the vaults of the gold given by the public
for the notes practically renders the note a mere
pawnbroker's ticket, a warrant for an article lodged,

and, as I have already shown, converts the notes into a metallic currency. Is not this a confession that a sound paper-currency is an impossibility; that it can be made sound only by ceasing to be in reality a paper-currency and becoming metallic? And is not such a confession a severe reflection on the civilization of our country and the resources of its intelligence and its science? Nay, is it not flatly and thoroughly refuted by the fact that the notes of the Bank of England and the notes of the Scotch bankers were universally recognized to be most excellent and trustworthy money, although in no sense metallic money? The substitution of paper money for coin is capable of conferring two great advantages on the nation—superior cheapness and superior convenience; but if the gold is purchased and kept in hand, one of these benefits, the cheapness, vanishes altogether. A 5*l.* note does identically the same work as five sovereigns: it costs a trifle, and the sovereigns cost one hundred shillings: unless, therefore, danger is proved to be not only theoretically possible, but practically existent and likely to be realized, it is pure folly and waste, as well as a humiliating disgrace to the state of civilization, to buy the expensive metal, as if the cheap paper were incapable of being used. That the cheap tool can be safely and beneficially employed, actual experience has demonstrated. To proclaim, therefore, as some of the defenders of the Act of 1844 do, that paper money can be made safe only by keeping the gold always on hand in the till, is a retrograde movement in the teeth of experience and science. It would be a confession of ignorance and stupidity voluntarily to abandon such a cheap and excellent instrument of currency under no prompting of danger, and to rush into a metallic currency from sheer want of intelligence. The Bank Act of 1844 can escape this severe censure only by pleading that the fifteen millions of uncovered notes are as large an amount as can safely be kept in circulation without coin in hand ready for payment on demand, and that the gold retained in the vaults is not an excessive reserve for the whole quantity of notes issued.

This plea is legitimate in principle. It reduces the discussion to the consideration of one single detail. On a circulation, say of twenty-eight millions, are thirteen millions of gold nothing more than the fitting and reasonable reserve required for securing the convertibility of the banknotes of the Bank of England? He would be a bold man who would assert this proposition categorically. What would he say to the fact that in 1825, when the severest run took place against the Bank, when country notes were dishonoured in shoals, and paper money was almost universally discredited, when too the reserve of gold had dwindled down to a million, the effort of the public was not to present the Bank of England notes for payment, but to procure them—to take them away home to their strong boxes, to hoard them as the best and safest investment of floating funds? On this occasion, the run on the Bank by its banking customers to withdraw their money was so severe that the Bank of England, in its character of banker, of a banker bound to give its customers their money back on demand, was saved from stoppage only by the accidental discovery of one million of unburnt one-pound banknotes. Those clamorous demanders of money had no fault to find with the

Bank's money. Whilst they refused to leave their means with the Bank, whilst they distrusted the Bank as the keeper of what was their own, they had the most implicit trust in the Bank's own money, in its solvency, in its being worth to them as much as the ringing sovereign which they were entitled to ask for. The Bank's money, the notes issued by the Bank, the mere pieces of paper in which the Bank acknowledged debts, were what they demanded, only they wished to have them in their own keeping. How can it be said, after that, that some ten or fifteen millions of gold are the necessary reserve of the Bank of England? This reserve does not even inspire a grain of additional confidence in the safety of the banknote; for the fact I have described indicates a confidence which is absolutely perfect. Neither has the severity of commercial crises been diminished by these vast stores of hoarded metal; for the violence of mercantile storms, the difficulty of procuring loans, the severity of the rate of discount have been as great with a minimum of eight millions as they were formerly with a minimum of one. Those who proclaim that gold is the averter of panics have contrived that the distressed City shall have seven millions at least of gold which it cannot possibly touch.

It is impossible, then, to justify, on grounds either of science or practice, the actual arrangement of the limit at which the issuing of notes uncovered by a deposit of gold should cease. The original figure of fourteen millions was taken at haphazard. No accurate and scientific examination preceded its selection. It chanced to be the sum due by the Government to the Bank, and the feeling apparently arose that by adopting this limit every note issued by the Bank would be covered. But the true question is, not only whether every note is safe, but also, at the same time, whether it is needlessly and excessively and therefore wastefully secured. I have repeatedly expressed the opinion elsewhere, that if experience were taken into account, and if it were remembered that the City has suffered as terrible agonies with the Bank's bullion at eight millions as when it stood at one million, twenty millions might be rationally substituted for fifteen millions as the point at which the storing of gold in the reserve should commence. The gigantic waste of purchasing with the wealth of the nation some seven millions of pounds' worth of a particular metal which can be put to no use, and can be of no more benefit than if it had remained in its Californian mine, would be avoided, whilst the soundness and convertibility of the note would not be in the smallest degree impaired. And I cannot but think that the teaching of experience would long ago have been listened to, and a modification which actual trial had warranted would have been introduced into the Act, had not this Act been valued as embodying ideas of a very different nature, and had not an unwillingness existed to endanger benefits to commerce, not the less highly prized because they were visionary and unreal. If the Act of 1844 were altered in this particular, and the limiting point moved up to twenty millions, it would, I conceive, be open to no important objection, whether scientific or practical.

The preceding discussion will have furnished an answer to a charge which has been brought against the Act of 1844 by the trading community with singular passion and vehemence. To this hour Chambers of Commerce angrily denounce it as restricting the supply of banknotes, and thereby diminishing the power of the Bank of England to make advances and grant other accommodation to trade. The charge is utterly unfounded. If traders wish to have a hundred millions of banknotes, they can have them. The Automaton will supply as many notes as people choose to ask for : only they must pay for them. The number of banknotes which the Automaton may issue is absolutely unlimited. The Act of 1844 does not breathe one word of restriction of numbers. It says only that if the public desires to purchase that convenient tool, a banknote, it shall have as many as it pleases, paying, however, for them as for any other tool which they may purchase in any of the shops of England In real truth, the Act of 1844 speaks, not of the quantity of notes which shall be issued to the public, but solely of the reserve of gold which shall be kept for paying them when presented for payment. It is simply and nakedly an Act for the regulation of the reserve. Omitting country notes, the fixing the point where the reserve shall begin is its one single provision. The amount of that reserve before 1844 was left to the discretion of the Directors of the Bank of England : it is now controlled by a fixed and self-acting rule ; and that is the whole of the matter. The authors of this statute and the traders who resent its enactments are under equal delusions respecting its action. It produces no effects whatever on the quantity of the circulation, on the numbers of the notes which the public employs ; and thus neither on the one hand does it

realize the dreams of those who would regulate the
circulation, and so, as they think, steady trade and
discount by legislative provisions, nor does it deprive
commerce of a single note which it may require.
It neither regulates nor restricts.

'This cannot be so,' the enemies and the friends
of the Act alike exclaim; 'it is disproved by the
necessity experienced in times of difficulty of sus-
pending the Act, and the manifest effect of such
suspensions. How can it be said that the Act does
not restrict, when veteran bankers and intelligent
merchants clamour for its temporary repeal when
trouble befalls the City, and when the repealing
Order of Council is found to bring healing on its
wings?' That suspension can calm the agitation
of the commercial mind, I have no difficulty in
admitting; but that suspension can or ever has
given any real relief to the distress of the money-
market, I deny. That a sick man may be soothed by
the administering of a phial of pure water, which he
believes to be a potent medicine, is a fact which
the practice of physicians attests; but is it the
water or the delusion which calms? If bankers
and merchants choose to believe that the suffering
of the money market comes from a want of banknotes, then, no doubt, it is easy to conceive that
the announcement that banknotes may be sent forth
without payment or limitation may buoy up their
imagination with the belief that the danger is
over, and that the impediments to borrowing have
passed away; but, assuredly, it is a mental and
not a material relief which will have been obtained.
Suspensions of the Act do not cure crises, and
for the very good reason that they cannot; it is

not in them to do it. Listen to Mr. Patterson,* speaking of the crisis of 1866: 'The panic was at its height at midday. Shortly before one o'clock the second edition of the daily papers appeared, containing an announcement that the Bank Act was suspended. A salutary change immediately became visible; Lombard Street became passable, and the crowds in the adjoining streets diminished. The run slackened; but the announcement was premature. The Bank Act was not suspended; nor indeed, at that time, as appears from the subsequent statements of the Chancellor of the Exchequer, had the Government given any attention to the matter. In this emergency, a deputation from the joint-stock and private banks was despatched to apprise the Government of the state of matters in the City, and to urge the immediate suspension of the Act of 1844. In the City, the managers and directors of banks and other monetary establishments remained at their post till past midnight, anxiously receiving the tidings of disaster, and waiting for the announcement of the suspension of the Act. It was midnight before the announcement was made. The effect of the announcement of the suspension of the Bank Act was so salutary, that next day (Saturday) it was generally thought that the crisis was at an end.'

Can picture be more graphic or more complete? The trembling fathers of the City, the agony, the terror at the ever closer approach of ruin, the waiting for the angel to come and trouble the water, the angel's arrival, and the instantaneous, the indescribable relief, are admirably painted; but the relief,

* The Science of Finance, p. 236.

was it a cure? Hear the next words of Mr. Patterson: 'But, as became visible in a day or two, the crisis was not at an end.' These are true words; the papers proclaimed the fact at the time. Why? asks Mr. Patterson. I cannot adopt his answer, for it is contradictory of my conception of currency. 'The Bank of England declined to avail itself of the power thus conferred upon it to extend its note-issues.' A shopkeeper does not decline to sell his goods, if his customers can pay for them. 'The Bank refused to extend its note-issues beyond the amount permitted by the Act of 1844,' for a reason with which we are all now, I trust, familiar—because they could not; because the enlargement of the issues of banknotes in no way rested with them but with the public only, and the public, even on that fearful day, had no desire for a single note beyond what it could procure without the suspension. As I have already explained, if the Bank had attempted, by its own act, to force on an extension of the issues; if it had said to the desperate borrowers, that they might have loans, if only they would carry them away in banknotes, the notes would have come in for payment to the Bank in an hour or two, for the simple reason that the wants of the borrowers were not for notes, and that their need had not created use for a single additional note. The extension could not, and did not, take place.

Events followed the same course in the crisis of 1847; the suspension of the Act did not lead to the issue of a single note beyond what the Act itself permitted. In 1857, a small excess of 800,000*l.* followed the suspension; so far the capacity of the public to hold notes and not to send them in for payment, exceeded the limits allowed by the Act. So far, then, the public would have lent funds to the Bank in exchange for notes. But the sum was trifling, and does not interfere with the conclusion that the suspension of the Bank Act did not as a fact relieve trade by an extension of the issue of banknotes.

You will ask, But how came the suspension to grant even a momentary relief? By acting on the feelings of two classes of persons, who believed in its efficacy to save. 'They thought,' as Mr. Patterson says, 'that the crisis was at an end,' and for the moment acted upon the supposition. Those bankers who had still means left for lending, but were hoarding them niggardly, were now warmed into a more generous handling of their treasures; the depositors at the banks and creditors generally were a little slower in demanding what was due to them. The suspension might touch feelings, but could not touch facts or the causes which had generated the crisis. Till a remedy had attacked these causes, they were certain to be at work again after the lull, and the disease was not cured. It could not be cured by banknotes; for neither banknotes nor gold had the remotest connection with the malady. Gold was not in demand; the Bank had never less than about twelve millions during the crisis. But the believers in the miraculous virtues of banknotes were not silenced; believers in the marvellous seldom are. They still replied in and out of Parliament that the suspension was inoperative, because it was clogged with a prohibition to the Bank not to lend at a lower rate than 10 per cent. The public, they contend, would have borrowed the notes, if they could have had them on cheaper terms. I will not linger over the strange notion that drowning traders would make difficulties in taking loans at 10 per cent.; but I will ask, What sort of Political Economy is it, which connects the rate of discount with the quantity of banknotes moving about the community? Why should the amount of the banknotes be more thought of in such a connection than the amount of corn, sugar, or cotton existing in England? Nay, does not the sale of these material substances, of that wealth, contain the causes of this eager desire to borrow and this hesitating disposition to lend; and are not banknotes but pieces of paper, which can only exchange commodities, but are not the commodities themselves nor wealth? Let me be forgiven if I remark that it would be well if great bankers, and merchants, and writers of City articles would study Political Economy a little; many delusions and some disasters might possibly be averted.

There remains a third method for securing the convertibility of the banknote, which has been largely adopted in America, and is warmly advocated by many bankers and traders in England. It consists in requiring the issuing bankers to place in the hands of the Government securities of a perfectly trustworthy character for the specific payment of the amounts pledged in the notes issued. These securities would naturally in most, probably in all, cases be composed of Government stocks, with an adequate margin to guard against fluctuations of their value in the market. Under such a system, the public would receive complete protection against loss, whilst the banker would derive a legitimate profit on his issues by means of the dividends accruing on the stocks which he had deposited with the Government. On the ground of science, I am not aware of any valid objection which can be urged against this method of guaranteeing convertibility. It would satisfy the one single claim which the public is entitled to advance in respect of banknotes, the complete solvency of the notes which circulate as money : that one condition fulfilled, the public has no right to inquire further into the matter. Many there are, indeed, who would shrink from an indiscriminate permission being granted to any one to issue notes at his pleasure ; but I have shown that the sole point of interest is the goodness of the note, its trustworthiness, its quality. If the notes are good notes, there is no reason, in the nature of the particular tool called a banknote, why it should not be sold in as many shops, why it should not be issued by as many bankers or private persons, as may have a fancy to put them forth. Who would say that any possible harm could come of every householder issuing sovereigns, if only the public had a complete guarantee that every one of these sovereigns was a good one ? The fundamental law always remains supreme, that the public cannot and will not keep more notes than its habits of life, its modes of buying and selling, can find use for ; and if too many shops were opened for the sale and issue of notes, those that put forth the excess would speedily find that their notes either did not circulate, or circulated in such small numbers as not to cover the expenses of the establishments of issue. As to the fear of prices and values being altered, it is perfectly idle, for the instant that the notes gave signs of depreciation they would be sent

in for payment, and, upon the supposition of the
securities lodged being ample, funds would be ready
for their payment. But, on the other hand, the same
consideration demonstrates that the hopes with
which Chambers of Commerce and many other
members of the commercial community advocate
the adoption of this system with so much passion
would be doomed to total disappointment. These
traders desire what they call unrestricted issues
under the belief that a freer emission of banknotes
would generate greater accommodation for them, freer
advances and loans, cheaper and more abundant discounting of bills; but they are not aware that the
number of notes circulating among the public is determined solely by the capacity of the public to
employ them, and that that capacity cannot be increased or diminished by the purely indifferent circumstance whether the notes are issued by one
banker or by a thousand. They might as reasonably
expect that the doubling of the number of grocers'
shops would double the consumption of tea.

But, on the score of practical working, this method
of issuing on the deposit of securities warrants a
certain degree of suspicion. Its virtue plainly depends on the goodness and sufficiency of these
securities, and it is very conceivable that many
Governments might be extremely lax as to what
securities they accepted, and what value they set
upon them. Unless the system were rigorously
administered, it would act as a snare, and lead to
evils far more dangerous than those which unguaranteed issues would be likely to produce in
our day. In the latter case, the public would know
that it was unprotected, and every taker of a note

would be conscious that he must exercise his own judgment as to the goodness of the note he accepts ; but, in the former, he would naturally believe that the solvency of the notes had been placed beyond danger before it came into circulation, and the failure of payment would come upon him afterwards as a cruel and unjustifiable surprise.

In connection with this portion of our subject, the question has been raised, and is still debated with much keenness both in England and France, whether the issue of paper money should be committed to one great establishment like the Bank of England or the Bank of France, or whether private persons may be legitimately entrusted with this semi-public function. An answer to this question will not be difficult for us. The principles of currency have nothing to say to this matter ; it is one of pure detail, of time and place, of local circumstances and habits. So long as the notes are good and sure to be paid, science is content, whether the issuers be few or many, whether the function be assigned to a great corporation or to individuals. As far as the science of currency is concerned, just as every man is at liberty to issue a cheque, so every man may be free to issue a note, if the guarantee for its redemption is sufficient. The nature of the guarantee is not one and universal ; a National Bank may become insolvent, and the notes of private issuers may never be tainted with dishonour. It is impossible to assert that any notes in the world have been better than the Scotch notes, even under the old system of unguaranteed issues and unregulated reserves. What objection can the principles of currency bring against them, so long as they fulfil the one vital

condition of solvency and convertibility ? And there
is always this advantage in favour of individual
issues, that they are proved by experience to cover
the land far more speedily and more effectually than
the notes of a central institution. The profits derived from these issues have contributed also to
the creation of banks, and their diffusion over the
country. If, then, banking is a good and desirable
thing, and the safe substitution of notes for coin
effects a great economy, it is difficult to refuse the
admission that private issues possess a certain superiority over central issues. On this point the remarks
of Mr. Gairdner, quoted in the Appendix, are exceedingly striking and important. Nevertheless, it cannot be denied that English country bankers showed
themselves by their multitudinous insolvencies to
be unfit to be entrusted with the responsible task
of putting forth paper money into the world ; and
the only conclusion we can arrive at, on the ground
of pure science, is, that the problem of the practical
issuing of notes must be left to the discretion and
administrative judgment of each nation, under its
own peculiar circumstances.

The same general considerations will furnish an
answer to another question which lies under great
misapprehension in England. Of what denomination
ought banknotes to be ? For how small a sum may
a banknote be issued ? I might reply by asking,
how small may a cheque be ? Why impose a limitation by law in the one case and not in the other ?
Every one sees that the limit applied to cheques is
one of convenience only. Very small cheques would
occasion great trouble to the bank ; they would
largely increase the number of entries in the bank's

books, would seriously multiply the labour of the
clerks, and, in a word, would generate an amount of
inconvenience which would be intolerable. The same
principle of convenience regulates the denomination
of banknotes, whatever currency writers may say on
the matter. In general, currency authorities have
a great horror of small notes; they see in them
unregu'ated, inflated, unmanageable issues in their
most intensified form. But we, who know that there
can be no such thing as inflation of perfectly convertible notes, need not be agitated by such alarms.
The suppression of one pound notes after the disasters of 1825 was an act of ignorance and panic.
It is too true that multitudes of innocent people
suffered cruel loss from the failures of the issuers of
one pound notes; but did not the hoarders of five
pound notes equally lose their money? The calamity
had not its origin in the denomination of the note,
but in the badness of the banking; though, on the
other hand, it must be freely admitted that the
sufferings of the poor, amongst whom these small
notes were widely distributed, merited in a special
degree the sympathy and the protection of the
Government. But if the evil has been cured at
its root, if the system of issuing furnishes a perfectly
trustworthy guarantee for goodness and solvency,
what possible rule but convenience can be found
for determining the denomination of the note? Two
and ten shilling notes work as successfully in Austria
as notes of thirty or three hundred. One pound
notes are a glory to Scotland at this very hour.
Mr. James Wilson, a very high practical authority,
proposed, I believe, ten shilling notes for India: on
what possible principle of science can objection be

taken against them? They may be found fault with, as troublesome, as difficult to count, as dirty and unpleasant to handle. These may be very legitimate objections, of which the public is the competent judge. It is no question of science. Doubtless, too, they can be more easily forged; and this is a practical reason of great weight. Still, it is not a reason derived from any principle of currency; it is a reason of mechanics, of manufacturing, on which a political economist need not dwell, when expounding the principles of currency.

It remains for me now to speak of inconvertible paper money—of banknotes which are not payable on demand, which receive a compulsory circulation from the law, and which, when once issued, must continue in the hands of the public, for the simple reason that those who are bound to pay are relieved by the law from the necessity of paying. It is very important here to have a clear understanding of the events which occur under such a system of currency. In the first place, how are such notes born into the world? How are they first brought into circulation? Occasionally, as in the case of our own Bank of England, a convertible currency, banknotes already issued under the obligation of being paid on demand, have been exempted by a subsequent special law from an immediate fulfilment of the pledge. But such an event is of rare occurrence. The almost universal origin of an inconvertible currency lies with the Government. A Government finds itself in want of resources; it seeks the means of buying, of procuring the articles which it wants. To obtain, like a banker, the funds of other people without giving anything in return but a mere acknowledgment of debt, a mere promise to pay, is a temptation to which many States have shown themselves to be accessible. The Government pays its debts, and makes purchases with these promises to pay, and then passes two enactments respecting them : first, that these promises to pay shall not be liable to be paid on demand ; and secondly, that they shall be a legal tender in the discharge of all debts and contracts throughout the land. And thus the question instantly arises—what effect does this exemption from immediate payment produce on the value of these inconvertible notes? Will a debt pledged to be repaid at twenty shillings, pass from hand to hand when no longer capable of claiming the twenty shillings on demand, or will it and must it suffer depreciation? Experience has proved that it need not of necessity suffer any depreciation of value; that it may still circulate at twenty shillings, in spite of being no longer a warrant which can be immediately converted into coin. For years after the passing of the Bank Restriction Act the notes of the Bank of England suffered no discount : at a later period, a guinea was worth twenty-seven shillings in notes.

How is this difference of effect to be explained? The general principles of currency, if you have fairly grasped them, will soon enable you to understand what occurs. You have seen that the public has a certain definite want for notes to use in the daily operations of buying and selling : there is a specific work to be done, and for that work it needs and will buy tools, precisely as a carpenter procures a basket of tools for the house that he is employed to build. For some portions of this work

the public purchases sovereigns; for other portions
it uses notes. Up to the full extent of this want,
of this demand, of this capacity to use notes, the
public will not send them in for payment, but retain
them, although it knows, when they are convertible, that it can at any time obtain sovereigns for
them in exchange. This being so, it is plain that
the prohibition to pay the notes can make no difference in the extent of the use which exists for the
notes: so far as this reaches, it is immaterial whether
the notes will or will not be paid on demand. The
only fact which could stop their circulation would be
their intrinsic worthlessness, for then they would be
altogether incapable of doing the work of money,—
they would be unable to give security to the man
who gave his goods for them, that he would be able,
by their means, to buy other articles of equal value
with those he had sold. This destructive feeling the
law always takes care to guard against by enacting
that these inconvertible notes shall be a legal tender
and effectual discharge of all debts. They become
good and serviceable notes then, in a measure; but
in what measure? to what extent? In the first
place, they are efficient tools, as good money as
convertible notes, provided that they are not issued
in greater numbers than the quantity of convertible
notes which would have been used, that is, provided
that their numbers are not larger than the public
can find employment for and hold. And remember
always carefully the meaning of this phrase,—that
the use and demand for notes are those exchanges,
that buying and selling, in which notes are actually
handled. In the early years, under the Bank Restriction Act, the Bank did not put more notes into

circulation than were required for this specific use : accordingly, the notes suffered no depreciation, for there was no cause at work to depreciate them. It was understood all along that the Bank recognized the notes as debts due by her to the public, though not to be paid for awhile ; and so long as the public really needed them, and would not have sent them in for payment had they been convertible, it did not matter a straw whether the day of payment was the day of their use, or a day a hundred years later.

But circumstances were radically altered when the Bank transgressed the limits of the real demand for notes, of the quantity which was actually needed for daily use. The difference of action between convertible and inconvertible notes then became instantly manifest. A convertible paper money encounters a most solid and objective obstacle to excess. The test, and a most real one it is, is instantly applied to superfluity ; the notes issued beyond the public wants are immediately sent back to the banker for payment. The vessel is full, and every additional note makes it to overflow. Convertible notes never can be in excessive circulation ; but inconvertible notes once placed with the public cannot be driven back. The issuing valve opens in one way only ; the excess remains amongst the public. What are the consequences of this fact, and by what rule are they measured ? The notes which surpass the demand become an article, of which the supply exceeds the demand ; they fetch a lower price, as every other commodity does under similar circumstances. Those who find themselves possessed of a larger quantity of these notes than they can use discover at the same time that they must make a sacrifice to induce others to take them in exchange for their goods. In other words, the notes fall to a discount, as when twenty-seven shillings of notes had to be given for a guinea of gold—or, which is the same thing, gold rises to a premium compared with the paper currency, as we now see happening in America. The American premium on gold does not indicate that gold, as such, has acquired a larger purchasing power; it is only another name for the discount attached to the greenbacks. The gold does not alter in value in America; it is the greenbacks only which suffer change.

What the causes are which regulate the actual amount of the depreciation, is a question which seems to me very hard to determine accurately. There is no difficulty with the same question in a metallic currency. There, the intrinsic value of the metal is the sole element which under ordinary circumstances governs its power of buying and exchanging. It is, as I have already explained, a matter of pure and direct barter. The cost price of the goods is compared with the cost price of the gold; and when the two are made equivalent, the bargain is struck, and the barter is carried out. If the cost price, therefore, of the gold were increased twofold, the coin would acquire a double purchasing power; if it were lessened ten times, ten times the quantity of metal would be required to purchase the same quantity of goods. But there is no intrinsic value, no cost price of a note, of a mere acknowledgment of debt, of a simple title to the delivery of an article of value, without the presence of any such article. No doubt the universal law of supply and demand applies to these trading tools, as to all others; but supply and demand are things subject to the most manifold and the most capricious differences. The only element of stability in the matter is the actual quantity of notes required for use in those transactions which are carried out by the agency of notes; and it may be, though I will not affirm that it is so, that if double the notes were issued, without any increase of buying and selling by means of notes, that the notes would sink to a depreciation of 50 per cent. There is for me, I confess, a certain obscurity as to the law which regulates the depreciation of inconvertible notes, which I have never been able to clear up to my satisfaction.

The question of the supply and demand of currency brings us face to face with Mr. Mill's central doctrine of money. 'The supply of money,' says Mr. Mill, 'is all the money in circulation at the time.' Nothing can be more true; but now let us look at the converse assertion. 'The demand for money,' he continues, 'consists of all the goods offered for sale. As the whole of the goods in the market compose the demand for money, so the whole of the money constitutes the demand for goods. The money and the goods are seeking each other for the purpose of being exchanged. They are reciprocally supply and demand for one another. It is indifferent whether, in characterizing the phenomena, we speak of the demand and supply of goods, or of the supply and demand of money. They are equivalent expressions. Hence, if the whole money in circulation was doubled, prices would be doubled; if it was only increased one-fourth, prices would rise one-fourth. The very same effect would be produced on prices if we suppose the goods diminished, instead of the money increased; and the contrary effect if the goods were increased and the money diminished. In the case of money, which is desired as the means of universal purchase, the demand consists of everything which people have to sell, and the only limit to what they are willing to give is the limit set by their having nothing more to offer. The whole of the goods being in any case exchanged for the whole of the money which comes into the market to be laid out, they will sell for less or more, exactly according as less or more is brought.'

The misconception involved in this view is thorough and fundamental. No wonder that after writing these words Mr. Mill complains of the complexity of the subject of currency and prices. They furnish a striking illustration of the truly wonderful facility with which even the most powerful intellects go astray on this fatal theme of currency. The misapprehension is the more remarkable, because no one has expressed many important truths about money with greater power and clearness than Mr. Mill. Yet even he himself has been unable to profit by the warning which he has given to others, or to escape the influence, as he describes it, of 'the lingering remnant of the old misleading associations, and of the mass of vapouring and baseless speculation with which this more than any other topic of Political Economy has in latter times become surrounded.' In laying the foundation of the explanation of the nature and action of money, Mr. Mill has failed to make an accurate analysis of the facts; and the result has been a confusion, which defaces this portion of his great treatise. That the money in circulation, including the necessary reserve stock provided to guard against fluctuations in its use, constitutes the supply of money, no one can doubt. That all goods for sale are estimated in money, and can be bought with money, is certain. That, further, some goods are actually exchanged for money, are bought and sold with coin and banknotes, is incontestable. But the fourth proposition, that all goods universally on sale, whether in a single country or all over the world, constitute the demand for money, and are seeking the thing called money, in the same definite sense that the drinkers of tea and wine constitute the demand for tea and wine and are seeking an actual supply of those specific articles, is not only not certain, but absolutely and glaringly untrue. Twenty thousand bales of cotton at New York are seeking to be sold and exported to England, and five thousand tons of iron at Liverpool are seeking to be sold to America. Both the cotton and the iron alike are estimated in money; they are on sale for money, they are offered for money, and if the sale is completed, they are sold in name for money. But does the money pass? Is the money produced in sovereigns or dollars on either side? Is the demand of the cotton and of the iron for money so real and specific, that the coin is produced, like wine is produced in bottles for the drinkers who desire to drink wine? Is this true? Is this the fact, the actual fact which goes on in the world? Is it not notorious that the cotton is sold for bills, which specify indeed sums of money, but which are only acknowledgments that no payment took place at the time of sale, and pledges that the payment shall be made at some future time? Purchasing by a bill is to take another man's' property without paying for it, the bill being merely legal evidence of the fact, and a foundation for an order of a court of law, if required, that payment shall be actually made. Is not the demand of the cotton and the iron for bills? Do not the owners of this cotton and of this iron say openly: 'We are demanding bills with this cotton and this iron : bills are what we seek. We are ready of course to give the cotton and the iron for money—for coin—if it is offered to us ; but we know that it will not be offered ; and, consequently, our demand is for bills, for promises of payment in the future, instead of a real payment in metal at the present moment. And what becomes of these bills? Are they paid in money when the stipulated period for payment arrives? Nothing of the kind. They are exchanged for one another ; the bills for the cotton are set off against the bills for the iron, and neither are paid in money. If the bills are not of exactly equal amount, the balance must be completed on the deficient side by a payment of metal, and this is the only money which is transmitted between the two countries in carrying out the vast purchases of the cotton and the iron. And thus the real fact becomes evident, that the cotton is exchanged for the iron, that the cotton buys the iron and the iron the cotton, and that a trifling addition of gold is made by the side which does not quite equal the calculated value of the other. The cotton must be calculated and expressed in money, and so must the iron, before they can be exchanged for one another ; in other words, they must be measured, and that is done by money ; but the actual money is not wanted at all, if the value of the cotton exactly equals the value of the iron. Such is the nature of the colossal trade which England carries on with foreign countries, and the same process goes on at home. The wine, the books, the clothes, the guns, are all seeking the consumers, who constitute their real demand; and they are given, for most transactions in England, not for money but for cheques. Neither in the home nor in the foreign trade is there any relation worth speaking of, none but a most insignificant one, between the goods set in motion by these trades, and the quantity of coin circulating about the world. Let the twenty thousand bales of cotton become fifty thousand, and the five thousand tons of iron swell into fifteen thousand; the goods for sale will then have been immensely increased, but so far from money being increased in the like ratio, if the iron still balances the cotton, not a single additional sovereign or dollar will be required to effect the sale. There will be no demand for the supply of a single additional ounce of gold or silver. The foreign trade of England can be, and probably is, at the present day, balanced by the same export of gold as was needed in the days when it had only one-fifth of its present size.

There is not the faintest trace in these enormous operations of commerce—operations which embrace in value almost the aggregate commerce of civilized nations in the modern world—of such a relation of demand and supply between money and goods as would connect any necessary increase or diminution in the use of money with an enlarged or diminished stock of goods offered for sale. Still less do we find any indication of that exact equality of ratio which

Mr. Mill alleges to exist between these two demands and supplies. He has sought for the demand for money in the wrong place, as will be obvious to those who have followed the analysis given in these Lectures, and consequently he has failed to find it. The true demand for money, as for every other commodity which men desire to purchase, consists in those requirements for money in which money is actually used. The tea-tables of England make up the demand for tea: the tea-drinkers seek tea, and use it: precisely in the same way, those particular sales and payments which are literally accomplished by money alone constitute the demand for money. There is a demand for money for travelling from London to Dublin: there is no demand for money, except perhaps a very trifling one, for purchasing the Cork butter which finds its way to Bristol. Let travelling increase, and co-operative associations with ready-money payments be multiplied, and the use and demand for money will follow the movement and expand proportionally. On the other hand, let banking and clearing-houses be diffused in larger numbers over the land, and the amount of the circulation and the need for money will infallibly decrease. The actual quantity of the goods sold, the size and importance of the trade, have no direct and necessary connection with the use of money. The manner of the buying and selling, the mode in which the goods are actually exchanged, is the vital point in determining how much or how little money shall circulate amongst the community.

'The whole of the goods in the market,' then, 'do not compose the demand for money.' What is it, then, that they demand? The demand of goods on

sale is a demand for other goods—a demand to be
exchanged, a demand of the seller for other commodities which he wants, in exchange for the super-
abundance of the goods he possesses and does not
personally want. A seller will accept money for his
goods, no doubt, because he knows that he can
exchange that money for the articles that he needs ;
but if any other instrument will accomplish this
purpose as well, he has no special desire or affection
for money, no real and specific need and demand for
it. As Mr. Mill excellently remarks : ' It must be
evident that the mere introduction of a particular
mode of exchanging things for one another by first
exchanging a thing for money and then exchanging
the money for something else, makes no difference
in the essential character of transactions. It is not
with money that things are really purchased. The
relations of commodities to one another remain unaltered by money.' Nothing can be more accurate
or more true. Money is not an end but a mean ;
and then, only one mean among many, one tool
amidst a stock of others. The farmer and the silk-
manufacturer seek to replace the articles which
their production has consumed ; and if they can
effect that replacement in any way their desire is
fulfilled. A bill or a cheque suits them perfectly ;
for though it is in reality no payment, still the
debt will be taken, directly or indirectly, by those
of whom they wish to buy, and their purpose is
answered. A transfer of a debt enables them to
procure a complete equivalent for their goods, and
they seek nothing more. No doubt, amongst the
other goods demanded by goods on sale, a certain
quantity of coin is included : for coin, money, is a

very useful tool, and for some few purposes indispensable; but the demand for this tool by the goods in the market is in every respect similar with the demand by these goods for guns and axes. The totality of the goods in the market is a demand not for money only, but for the totality of all articles required for use. And thus we arrive, at last, at the true view, that money is a tool required for certain specific purposes—that all the goods in the market contain a demand for this tool inclusively with all the other tools and conveniences of civilized life, and that the number of this tool really demanded—the demand which regulates the supply—is composed of those specific transactions in which it is employed. These transactions, these payments made with money, have no direct or organic relation to the totality of the goods on sale, be it large or be it small. In some countries, those which are relatively uncivilized, the ratio will be a large one, for barbarous nations require real payment, and have little faith in such deferred payments as bills, cheques, and banknotes. On the contrary, in those civilized countries where banking is largely practised, that ratio will be an exceedingly small one. When the quantity of money needed for these payments is supplied, money, as I have already explained, will share the fate of all other commodities. If it is produced in excess of this want, its value must inevitably fall; and if the cost of mining will not admit of its being produced at a reduced price, the operations for extracting gold from mines will be contracted. This is the whole of the matter; and there is no mystery or obscurity about it.

Mr. Mill has also spoken much of credit; and

at the outset he has made a statement of exceedingly great value. 'I apprehend,' says he, 'that banknotes, bills, or cheques, as such, do not act on prices at all. What does act on prices is credit, in whatever shape given, and whether it gives rise to any transferable instruments capable of passing into circulation, or not.' This is a fundamental truth of immense importance in currency: it kills off at once a multitude of empty theories about inflations of banknotes, which expand the circulation, and swell prices, and engender crises, and smite the commercial world with desolation. I would, however, substitute for Mr. Mill's word another of wider range. What raises prices universally is buying, whether that buying be made by the transfer of an article of equivalent value, such as coin, or whether the goods are sold and delivered without payment being made at the time. The greater the buying, either on trust or with coin, the stronger will be the tendency of the articles in demand to rise in price. The particular manner in which evidence is obtained of goods having been delivered without payment, and security taken, by bill or note, that this deferred payment shall in due time be effected, is utterly insignificant, as far as concerns any action on prices. Credit, no more than purchases with coin, does not create capital; it only places the disposal of a pre-existing capital in new hands. Banks and financial companies of all kinds neither create nor handle capital, save the small change of coin which they actually use. They may produce vast good by giving the power of purchasing capital to persons who can make a profitable use of it, and apply it to the creation of wealth, or they may give the command of it to men who will waste and destroy it; but the instruments by which this transfer of purchasing power is bestowed are mere machinery: they are not the substance itself. They are not capital, they are not even indispensable for its transfer; for a vast amount of lending and borrowing may go on by means of word of mouth only, and may generate the identical effects produced by what are called instruments of credit. Goods bought by a spoken order, of which the seller makes an entry in his books, may enormously surpass in quantity those purchased by coin or paper instruments of exchange; and of this fact Mr. Mill has given the most striking illustration. It would be well, therefore, to bear in mind constantly, that the danger involved in credit, as compared with purchases with coin, is the facility thereby given to a buyer to obtain goods which he has not the means to pay for, and the danger thus brought on the seller of losing his property altogether. Credit implies an engagement to pay at a later period; and if credit has been too profusely accorded, if buyers have been carelessly allowed to take goods away without satisfactory assurance being given of their future ability to pay for them, loss must ensue, and it may easily be expanded into crisis and ruin. At such a period, no doubt, as Mr. Mill has well explained, an immense collapse of prices may follow on a rise artificially created by an excess of speculative buying; but this will be an event of pure trading only, and not of currency. Not a bill or a cheque may have passed; and yet all, or almost all, the disasters might have equally occurred.

But Mr. Mill proceeds further subsequently, and

combines with his principle that it is credit which
acts on prices, such a view of the action of banknotes, bills, or cheques, as to bring himself at last
into something like contradiction with the general
statement which I have quoted. At least it becomes
necessary for him to modify it, and to make it declare
that though it is credit, and not banknotes, bills, or
cheques, which as such acts on prices, nevertheless
these tools of credit may work in such a way as
to augment or diminish credit, and thereby act indirectly on prices. He raises the question whether
'any particular mode or form of credit is calculated
to have a greater operation on prices than others,
by giving greater facility or greater encouragement
to the multiplication of credit transactions generally;'
and this question he is disposed to answer in the
affirmative. He says very truly, that 'if banknotes
or bills have a greater effect on prices than book
credits, it is not by any difference in the transactions
themselves, which are essentially the same, whether
taking place in the one way or the other. It must
be that there are likely to be more of them,—that
is, more transactions, more buying upon credit, and
consequently a rise of price in commodities, as being
in greater demand. If credit is likely to be more
extensively used as a purchasing power, when banknotes or bills are the instruments used, than when the
credit is given by mere entries in an account, to that
extent and no more there is ground for ascribing to
the former a greater power over the markets than
belongs to the latter.' He then affirms, that 'there
appears to be some such distinction.'

Mr. Mill finds the proof of this distinction in the
fact, 'that if A has given B a bill for the amount

of the goods he has purchased of him, B can get the
bill discounted, which is the same thing as borrowing
money on the joint credit of A and himself; or he
may pay away the bill in exchange for goods on the
same joint credit. In either case here is a second
credit transaction grounded on the first, and which
would not have taken place if the first had taken
place without the intervention of a bill.' Mr. Mill
further urges with entire truth, that a bill or a banknote is a 'more potent' instrument for borrowing
than a simple entry in a book-account; for undoubtedly it is more easy for two persons, other
circumstances being the same, to borrow conjointly,
than for one. But is it certain that a second credit
transaction is created by the use of a bill, which
would not have taken place without the bill?
B, the seller of the goods to the speculator A, is
not necessarily himself a speculator; and it may
very well happen that he will not acquire an additional power of borrowing by having a bill with
A's name upon it than if he employed solely his own
personal credit. However, it is possible that the
second name of A may enable B to borrow more
easily, and so to perform a second act of credit;
but I conceive the case to be quite otherwise with
banknotes. Before any use can be made of banknotes, they must be previously bought and paid for:
so that in this case A, paying not with a bill but
with banknotes, is not making a new transaction
of credit. Nor can the banker increase such transactions by additional issues, for I have shown that the
banker's power to issue notes depends entirely on
the powers of the public to hold the notes and its
willingness not to send them in for payment; and

A's application to the banker for notes does not increase this power of the public to hold the notes, and, in truth, has no manner of connection with it whatever. A can procure notes solely by purchasing them; and the payment he gave, whether by goods or otherwise, to obtain the notes, constitutes a real equivalent of his subsequent purchase from B, and prevents it from being an act of credit. An act of credit no doubt took place when the banker first got the notes into circulation; but years may have elapsed since that event happened before that A bought them and used them as an instrument for buying from B.

Before leaving this part of my subject, I beg to make one quotation more from Mr. Mill, because it states a most significant fact, and strongly corroborates the principle on which I take my stand, that the amount of notes in circulation depends exclusively on the number required by those transactions in which notes are used, together with the stock needed to meet fluctuations in their use. 'The banknote circulation of Great Britain and Ireland,' says Mr. Mill, 'seldom exceeds forty millions, and the increase in speculative periods, at most, two or three millions.' This is exactly what we ought to have expected upon general reasoning *à priori.* The difference in the amount of the circulation caused by a crisis is trifling, and is amply explained by the fact, that at seasons of commercial alarm, bankers all over the country increase their reserves, and demand an augmented supply of notes from the Bank. Two or three millions may be easily required for these reserves; but you will observe that this is the maximum which such increase of the circulation attains amidst such difficulties, and that very frequently, as City writers have observed with astonishment, the limits of the ordinary circulation are not exceeded. In the presence of such a fact, what has the City to say in defence of its vehement demands for the suspension of the Bank Act of 1844, its outcry for more notes, its vehement complaints of restriction, its loud demands for free banking, as the saviour of trade by the healing power of unlimited issues ? Two or three millions of notes out of forty is the supreme boon which the practical man can provide for afflicted commerce. Three parts out of a hundred of the operations of banks, according to the testimony of Sir John Lubbock, is the field of action on which his intelligence tells him that this miracle of salvation is to be effected !

LECTURE VI.

THE MONEY MARKET AND GOLD.

WE have seen in the preceding Lectures that various instruments are employed by civilized nations for carrying out the great function of exchange. Coin, banknotes, cheques, bills, and not unfrequently post-office orders and postage-stamps, are all used for the same end. They all perform the same identical work with mere modifications of detail, each in its own sphere, according to its nature; coin and banknotes where the buyer is unknown, the several forms of paper currency where large sums are to be moved about, bills in the conduct of foreign trade, and so on, as the varying circumstances of buying and selling may require. They all buy property and pay debts: they all serve one purpose and one purpose only, the transmission of the ownership of wealth from hand to hand. There is no difference of any kind in the essential character of the common function which they all discharge; but each, whether from its intrinsic value, its lightness, the security it gives against robbery, its cheapness, the ease with which it is created, or the facilities furnished to it

by law for negotiation and transfer from one owner
to another, has a natural fitness for being employed
rather than the others in the purchases and payments
for which it is especially adapted. But although
they all perform the same work, are they all to be
called money? That coin is money, no one disputes:
money is the original word devised for the circulating
medium, as it is called, which in civilized countries
is composed of some kind of coin. We have been
compelled to apply the same term 'money' to banknotes; and I have shown that their right to this title
consists in the fact that they circulate, taken in combination with their impersonal character. These two
qualities impart to banknotes a resemblance to coin
so strong as to necessitate their being included under
the same designation of money. The common language of the world has adopted this extension of the
word money; and the ideas associated with coin and
banknotes are too similar, and the fact of their general
circulation is too strong, to allow of any attempt
being made to call them by different names without
producing hopeless confusion.

But are the other instruments of exchange which
I have enumerated money? If we do not wish to
render a science of currency impossible by running
into utter vagueness, these tools for effecting exchanges, for making purchases and payments, must
not be regarded as money. They do not circulate—
and that is a perfectly sufficient reason for drawing
a broad line of distinction between them and the two
familiar varieties of money, coin and banknotes.
They are not taken by the general public; they are
personal in their nature; their value is known to
rest on the trustworthiness of one or two personal

signatures, and every man who accepts them as payment is fully aware that the duty lies on him to assure himself beforehand of the certainty of their being paid on demand. We thus reach the division of the instruments of exchange into Money and Not-Money ; and this is a valuable distinction, because there are certain attributes of money, certain precautions to be provided for its use, certain consequences to be drawn from its peculiar qualities, which are of great importance for science and for practice. Nevertheless, I have long felt that another classification, a classification founded on a different principle, was eminently desirable for an easier and more thorough understanding of the subject of currency. Its foundation would be a great truth, which cannot be kept too carefully in view. The distinction I would suggest would place coin in a class by itself, and would group in a second and collateral class all the other instruments of exchange. The two classes of the instruments of exchange would then be guarantees by a commodity and guarantees by account. The basis of this division is the fact that coin constitutes an actual payment. It places in the hands of a seller an article of equal intrinsic value with the goods he is parting with : the guarantee which such a seller possesses, that he will be able to obtain other commodities of the same value as those he sold, is perfect, because he holds a commodity, a metal, of a definite exchangeable value in the market. In this respect, the other instruments of exchange, cheques, bills, banknotes, post-office orders, stand on a totally different basis. They do not pay, but only promise and pledge themselves to pay. They are orders to give money, to hand over coin—*titres*, as the French say, to the delivery of metal, legal evidence of debt, which the law, if required, will enforce; but till the metal, the coin stipulated for, is delivered, they are only pieces of paper, and nothing more. They stand on a level with the entries in a shopkeeper's books. They are matters of account—debts, whose payment is deferred, and which, though perfectly sure to be paid at last, are debts only. This distinction then is real and founded on fact, and furnishes an excellent foundation for the classification of the instruments of exchanges into guarantees by means of a commodity, and guarantees of account.

I do not for a moment suppose that it is possible to supersede, much less to obliterate, the use of the word money: the attempt to do this would be an absurdity. The word money is rooted in the language of all nations; and the necessity will always remain for the expounder of science to distinguish, amongst the instruments of exchange, between Money and Not-Money. But it will scarcely be denied that a very important advantage will be gained if, in the study of the science of currency, the student is made familiar with a division, which is at once real, and brings also into marked prominence the two fundamental ideas, that all forms of currency are in their nature guarantees, and that the transfer of a debt from hand to hand effects, in the vast majority of transactions, the work of exchanging goods for goods as successfully and as safely as the delivery of a piece of valuable metal. Certainly it is my own strong conviction that the views entertained on this branch of Political Economy would be wonderfully altered for the better, both in respect of accuracy and

clearness, if the habit were general to speak of money
and bills and cheques as guarantees to a seller for
obtaining the goods he wants to an equal value with
those he sold. Nor would the gain be less in the
habitual use of the word 'account.' A cloud of mis-
conceptions would vanish before these two words.
No one has currency theories about the debts which
shopkeepers have in their books against their customers; no one speaks of an inflation of shopkeepers'
accounts, of a contraction of tradesmen's debts as
bearing on the rate of discount or the supply of
means to bankers or others for making advances to
merchants. It would be like the clearing out of a
high road through an Indian jungle, if the words
daily, or at any rate scientifically used, brought
instantly and naturally to the mind the perception
that one instrument alone effects payment, inasmuch
as it alone gives a commodity intrinsically worth the
goods it purchases, and that all the rest mean simply
getting goods on trust without paying for them at
the time.

The word money has been singularly maltreated by
the daily language of the world. It started with a
most sharply-defined and accurate meaning, the 'coin
of the realm,' the pieces of gold, silver, and copper by
which purchases were made in the market, and the
debts of all were discharged. It suffered some degree
of violence when it was extended to banknotes, to
pieces of paper which were destitute of all intrinsic
value, which put no equivalent merchandize into the
hands of a seller, and were thus separated by an
enormous gap from the substantial and saleable
qualities of the precious metals. Yet the extension
was not without justification; for there were points

of resemblance in their modes of action between coin and banknotes, which naturally placed them in the same category. But what are we to say of expressions such as these? 'Money is dear to-day, and money is cheap; there is plenty of money, and money is very scarce.' How is it possible for the City, when it is in the daily habit of uttering such expressions, to escape from falling into a multitude of unreal and incongruous ideas? How can a man who every day of his life is saying that money is abundant and cheap, or money is scarce and dear, avoid associating with what he calls the rate for money the quantity of money moving about the town? He gets established in his mind a ratio in money between quantity and price. And what renders the absurdity complete is the fact that all the time no money, so to speak, passes at all—that money, in all these operations, is a mythical shadowy personage, who is much spoken of, but is hardly ever seen or handled—whose presence is ever promised and pledged but is most rarely discerned by the hand or the eye. The City is a most difficult country for Political Economy to penetrate. The mischief would be comparatively trifling· if these mutilated and perverse expressions were confined to the particular occurrences in which they had their origin, if these uses of the word money were limited to the description of the abundance of means at bankers', and the prices which they charge for discount. But the evil becomes very serious when the ideas generated by this language implant the thought deep in the minds of merchants and traders, that a large quantitative supply of gold and banknotes is the essence of trade, and that their operations ought to be regulated by the signs which indicate that this supply will be forthcoming. And then when times of difficulty arise, when bankers are pressed for loans, and great firms succumb under the weight of disaster, the force of these ideas drives merchants into seeking help, in quarters empty of all relief, and the nation and its Parliament is involved in idle discussions, which can be productive of no good, because they are founded on the misapprehensions set afloat by the misapplication of the word money. The commercial mind is thus trained to confound wealth with the tools by which its ownership is transferred from one person to another, and from this root every kind of misunderstanding shoots up in profusion.

Money, true money, is neither abundant nor scarce, whilst the rate of discount ranges over the widest intervals; the stock of gold will probably have remained unchanged, and the alterations in the stock of banknotes presented insignificant changes by the side of the gigantic variations in the situation of the City. Nor is it money which is dear or cheap when the rate of interest is at ten per cent. or at two; for the dearness or cheapness of money are the dearness and cheapness of the metal of which it is composed, and of nothing else. Money was dear six centuries ago, because the cost of producing gold and silver from the mines was very heavy, and miners could not afford to go on with their mining unless large portions of other goods were given to them in exchange for very small bits of metal. Money is cheap now, because the resources of modern civilization have placed immense means at the disposal of miners, and the metals are extracted from the depths of the earth with an ease which

enables the workmen to give large pieces of their
metals for other kinds of wealth. What the City
really means by money being cheap or dear is that
loans of money are made on dear or easy terms ; but
they do not play tricks with language with impunity.
The confusion which afflicts the City on all matters
connected with the scientific understanding of money
is the penalty which they pay for the abbreviations
which they find so convenient, and I have shown how
severe it is in its consequences.

The looseness of the City's language reaches its
climax in that remarkable phrase, 'the money market.' How pleasant is the alliteration, how easily
it flows ! Yet what is the meaning of this smoothly-
running combination of words ? What is the money
market ? It is easy to say what it is not. It is
not a market for money—a place in which money,
sovereigns, and banknotes are specially sold. There
is very little of the money circulating about England
to be found in the City. There is only one spot
within its boundaries in which it exists in large
quantities—in Threadneedle Street ; yet the stores
which are piled up there are not brought to market.
The hoards of ingots which the law of 1844 com-
mands to be piled up against the issue of banknotes
are not for sale ; they cannot be handled and put
on the counter, and be passed over to any purchaser. They are sentenced, for the most part, never
to see the light of day ; their destiny, whatever
else it may be, is not to be brought to market.
The other supplies of money, the banknotes and
sovereigns which are bought and sold in the City,
can boast of no extraordinary numbers relatively
to the remainder of the kingdom. There are more

notes and sovereigns in London than in Manchester, because there is a larger number of transactions, just as there is a larger corn trade. There is no spare quantity of these tools in London, in such abundance as to constitute the City in any degree the market for money.

What, then, I repeat, is the 'money market?' What does a City man understand by the expression? It is impossible to answer the question by a single phrase. It is a noun of multitude: it gathers up under one title many diverse and even heterogeneous things: it is a label put upon a drawer containing a great variety of different papers. The business of the Stock Exchange would, I presume, be called a part of the money market; yet of what multiform elements is it composed! Cast your eyes down one of its daily lists. What first meets the eye? The quotations of the prices of railway shares. Yet a railway company has no particular connection with money. Railways are mere carriers, and scientifically no distinction, but of detail, can be drawn between them and the common country carrier going his rounds with his slowly-moving horse. But railways are public companies, and what is quoted is the sum of money for which a share in this property may be purchased. But public companies are not a necessary part of the money market: there are probably many hundreds, perhaps thousands, of public companies in England, that is, trading associations of at least seven persons working under a particular Act of Parliament, whom no one would dream of including in the money market. So it is with the mines and all kinds of miscellaneous properties enumerated in the list of the Stock Exchange: they are trading bodies and nothing more. But what shall we say of Government stocks? of consols and foreign funds, and other national securities? Are they not money; and are not dealings in them dealings in money? But if these questions are to be answered in the affirmative, must we not equally call every annuity granted by an assurance company a part of the money market? Public funds are only annuities: the only fact they contain is the annuity covenanted to be granted by a Government. The price quoted for consols is only the sum which a buyer is ready to give for 3l. a year. All these matters united help us but a very little way to the understanding of the term 'money market.' We shall gain more light from an explanation which has sometimes been given to the phrase by calling it the Loan and Investment market. There can be no doubt that loans constitute the most important and the most characteristic feature of the money market, yet something more is needed before the root of the matter can be reached. There are many loans and investments made daily, which are far beyond the limits of the money market: investments in the purchase of lands and houses, loans granted on mortgage, purchases of shares in every kind of commercial business, which in the aggregate probably far exceed the transactions which the money market can fairly claim for its own.

The real kernel of the phrase is to be sought rather in those unappropriated funds, of which bankers and financial institutions are the principal depositaries. The word 'money market' has its most direct reference to the loans granted by bankers, and the rate of interest which they charge for these advances; and as trade, and most of all foreign trade, is carried on by the help of these funds, lent on the discounting of bills, the supply of this money, as it is called, of these means of buying, of this purchasing power, as we should say, acquires vast importance. This is the true money market, whose state it is essential for so many traders to understand, so as to estimate the probabilities of borrowing becoming more easy or more difficult, more cheap or more dear. Only, merchants are beguiled into supposing that these means of lending exist in the form of money, in tangible sovereigns and banknotes, and seem to have no consciousness that they are composed of debts, of lines in ledgers, of purchasing power acquired by the sale of commodities, of debts due by the stock of goods in the country, and transferred by the bankers to traders who wish to buy merchandize through their agency. Money, real, true money, plays no part worth mentioning in these operations: and it is a practical misfortune that merchants, by the use of such phrases as cheap and scarce money, money market, and the like, should have their attention diverted from the causes which govern the supply of these funds, and fixed on a few tools which serve only one particular and subordinate purpose.

But the greatest of commercial delusions is the wonderful apostasy about gold. I call it apostasy, because the light was made to shine, and men wilfully shut their eyes against it. Adam Smith exposed in undying words the emptiness and the absurdity of that inveterate fallacy of the trading world which has been called the Mercantile Theory.

Many writers of great ability followed him in
the same path, and this famous theory became
almost a by-word for ridicule. Men for a time were
shamed out of such a preposterous illusion, but for
a time only. Truth in this region proved itself to
be no match for error: the tendency to backslide
into the old thoughts, into the old habit of looking
only at what was visible and on the surface, was
irresistible. Money buys goods, with money debts
are paid, money opens shops and warehouses, loans
and advances are counted in money; therefore money
is the true riches, money is the one thing of which
there never can be too much, money is the soul
and essence of all trade, money is the wealth of
nations. Such is the universal, the indestructible
doctrine—the lowest level to which all mercantile
ideas gravitate, the obvious, practical, intuitive truth
which no dissertations of philosophers will ever be
able to shake or overturn. Gold, therefore, is the
true divinity which traders must worship; gold is
the best, the ultimate end of all their efforts. That
is a prosperous trade for a nation which brings
in a balance of gold: a trade which results in a
permanent export of gold cannot fail to impoverish.
Exchanges, therefore, which indicate that the foreigner
is sending gold to a nation, are called favourable:
exchanges which imply that gold is leaving the
country are viewed with general uneasiness, and
are held to require the immediate application of
corrective measures. But not only is the general
principle certain that the value of a trade is measured
by the balance of imported gold which it yields,
but the subordinate position is also indubitable that
the money market, the power of lending and bor-

rowing, experiences ease or difficulty according as
the daily operations of commerce bring in supplies
of the precious metal. Such is the established theory
of trade at the present day; and it is worked out
with great zeal by a vigorous literature, which
diffuses itself daily over all Europe. The City
articles of all the newspapers of the world are satu-
rated with the Mercantile Theory. Their writers
have probably never read a line of Adam Smith's
works: not a trace of his influence can be discerned
in their articles. He is not even thought to be
worth refuting. Reflecting men have not the con-
solation of seeing a counter view to Adam Smith's,
built up by careful argument: such a process is not
even attempted. It would have been a satisfaction
to know that at least the capacity to reason had not
been smothered; but what care writers of City
articles for the investigation of first principles? Do
they not stand on the solid fact, that gold can buy
and pay debts, and is not that enough? Is it not
easier and more intelligible to say at once, that some
fifty thousand pounds were taken to the Bank to-day
and a quieter tone prevailed in the money market,
or that a hundred thousand were drawn out for
exportation and advances were not so easy?

I confess that I never address myself to the examination of such language without some feeling of
humiliation: to have to repeat Adam Smith's refutation of the Mercantile Theory to the whole trading
world, in an age remarkable for intellectual activity,
is a spectacle far from gratifying to the believers in
the power of truth and genius. How can one hope
for the victory of truth when an exploded delusion
can re-appear in such force, and assert its mastery

over a whole community? what confidence can be placed in [the success of new arguments, when reasoning of the most powerful order has served only to flash a brief outbreak of light, to be followed after by darkness more universal, more deeply settled down than ever? The task would be far more easy and more agreeable if one had to encounter systematic argument, if the despisers of Adam Smith stood on ground which they ventured to assert as their own. But a simple collapse into a gross superficial view, unsupported by any scientific investigation, or any analysis of first principles distinctly enunciated and consistently defended, is difficult to deal with; for reasoning and science produce no effect on minds which have sunk into such a condition.

The attempt, however, to induce traders to think out the principles which underlie their practice, must be made: and first of all, I would ask them to state plainly and distinctly what they conceive to be the object for which gold is imported into England. I ask for a direct, downright, categorical answer to this question. Gold is not produced in England: it must be bought from abroad: it has to be paid for with English goods, the fruit of English labour and English capital. English wealth must be given away to acquire this gold; for what purpose, I repeat, is this very costly article purchased by English merchants? In this discussion, the use of gold in the making up of jewellery and other wares does not come under consideration: we are speaking here of gold in its relation to universal trade. Wine is imported to be drunk, silk to be worn, indigo for dyeing, and so on; but what does the City think that gold is bought and imported for? My own answer to the question is easy and direct; but it would little satisfy the City and writers of City articles. I say that gold is bought and imported to circulate as sovereigns, with the necessary reserve stock that is required for all articles of variable consumption. Sovereigns are excellent tools for certain special work, and as such confer great benefits on society. They are as directly useful in the production of wealth as saws, or looms, or factories. It is essential that a country should have a full supply of these tools, and they are worth all the wealth which it costs to buy them. It is a good and useful exchange to part with some English wealth in return for these Australian sovereigns: the sum total of the wealth of England is ultimately increased by the operation. For me, this explanation of the object for which it is desirable to import sovereigns is exhaustive; but it cannot be so for City men and newspaper writers, for it would speedily land them in the necessity of confessing that when this purpose of circulating is satisfied, when there are sovereigns enough to do this work of buying and selling, all motive for importing more gold ceases. That confession would be the ruin of the Mercantile Theory and of all those who think that the grand point is always to import and never to export gold.

So again I ask the question, what do these writers assert to be the purpose, over and above this supply of the requisite quantity of circulating sovereigns, for which it is desirable to buy and import gold? I am not acquainted with any such purpose; and I cannot find any distinctly and plainly described by these lovers of the importation of gold. They would admit, I may presume, that if all the labourers of England were employed in the conversion of all her capital into goods to be exchanged for gold to be imported from abroad, all Englishmen would speedily be reduced to nakedness and starvation. They must allow of necessity that there is a point at which there is gold enough in England, and that beyond that point the importation of this metal is the importation of a perfectly useless thing—as useless as would be a cargo of stones—and that the wealth which it cost to purchase would be for the time annihilated, and its exportation a dead loss to England. This being undeniable, what is this point? I ask. Upon my view, that point is the full supply of sovereigns required for use, with the necessary stock for fluctuations in this use: and I go still further, and assert that ever since 1819 the supply of gold in England has always been in excess of this demand for use, and that she has all along since that period had more gold than she has known what to do with. Men cannot wear sovereigns, or eat them, or drink them: ingots are not ends, final objects of consumption: they can be employed only as means to effect some ulterior purpose; and the bullion laid up in store in the vaults of the Bank of England have been as wasteful and useless purchases as would have been docks full of timber for which there was no demand. And since bullion is not applied to direct consumption, and since when there are sovereigns enough for carrying out the buying and selling, for which they are the actual tools employed, more cannot be used as capital, it follows irresistibly that this bullion, not being consumable wealth nor capital, is practically and substantially not wealth at all, and forms no more a portion of the nation's riches than the fertility of a field which is never cultivated. I hold this demonstration to be as complete as any in Euclid, and its force cannot be resisted, except by denying its premiss, that the employment of gold as sovereigns in circulation is the sole utility derived from the gold which merchants affirm to be the grand object of trade to import. If, therefore, the City and the newspapers desire to escape the destructive cogency of this reasoning, let them tell the world plainly what benefit, other than that of the supply of working sovereigns, this imported gold affords.

It is not sufficient to reply, as many do, that with gold everything may be bought, and that the merchant who can obtain possession of gold has the command over every shop and every warehouse. To acquire this command, it is not necessary to send English wealth away in order to procure the new instrument of exchanging. Gold buys, no doubt, but so does every other piece of saleable goods in market; and gold buys but a very trifling portion indeed of the merchandize actually bought and sold. Not to know that all trade is an exchange of commodities, and that all buyers, whether nations or individuals, buy with their own goods, is to be ignorant of the first rudiments of Political Economy. The rich landowner, with a gigantic rental, buys with the share of the corn, hay, and animals which accrues to him in the business of farming. The tenant, no doubt, pays his rent either in money, or more commonly with a cheque; but that is only because he is at the trouble of selling the landlord's share of the produce of the farm. The landlord's income is none the less on that account his

part of the results of the manufacture of corn and
meat carried on upon his land. The bullion sleeping
at the Bank—bullion which may wake up never, if
the law of 1844 remains unchanged—does not give
a single person in the kingdom the power of buying
one shilling's worth of commodities beyond what
could and would have been bought had the metal
continued to lie undisturbed in its Californian bed.
In truth, the supposition is simply ludicrous, that a
Lincolnshire farmer and a London gunmaker cannot
exchange a horse for a gun without buying foreign
gold to effect the operation. It is this fact, that gold
is bought and paid for, which a City man and a
writer of City articles find it so hard to bear in mind.
The power of the gold to buy is always present to
their minds. The equal power of the goods sent
abroad to procure the gold is forgotten; and the
diminution of English capital by the purchase of a
tool which is not wanted, and whose work can be
efficiently performed without it, never occurs to their
thoughts. Of the two, the City merchant is more
excusable than the article writer; for it is his object
to obtain profits from his business, and profits are
always estimated in money, and as a seller in foreign
countries, he is perfectly satisfied if the produce of
his venture is brought home to him in a saleable
metal. The article writer professes to think and to
theorize, for he seeks to explain and to guide; and
it is difficult to conceive how it comes to pass that so
obvious a fact that goods are purchased by other
goods should, whenever he speaks of gold, be so
completely pushed out of sight. Till he can tell the
world, in plain intelligible language, what end the
treasures whose arrivals he delights to record serve,

what utility they bring, when they flood a quantity of sovereigns already sufficient for their work, he is but a blind leader of the blind. The very circumstance which he announces, that the gold is taken to the Bank, of itself alone ought to have opened his eyes to the uselessness and the waste of this importation that he urges his commercial readers to exult over: for a spot more shut out from the life of the world, more identical with the deep Australian mine, than the vault of the Bank of England, cannot well be imagined.

But the stronghold at the present day of the pre-eminent importance of gold is banking and the ideas associated with it. Bankers are very sensitive about their reserve, especially in critical times; and they seem seldom able to divest themselves of the feeling, that an abundance of gold in the country means plenty of gold in their reserves. Hence their tendency to watch the movements of this metal, and, if report is to be believed, to regulate the rate of interest, according as gold may be ebbing or flowing. This feeling quietly propagates itself amongst merchants and traders, who rely for the conduct of their business on the funds which they obtain from banks; and thus the whole commercial community gets to believe that life or death lies in the abundance or the scarcity of gold. I have already shown at length that a banker's funds are composed of debts, which he receives from one person and lends out to another; and that his reserve, his stock of unlent money, is regulated by the ratio which he keeps between his receipts and his lendings. I have again and again pointed out, that since 1819 gold has never been deficient in England; that those who

o

could pay for a supply of the metal) have always been
able to procure it : and if this is so—and I believe
it to be incontestable, for I have never been able to
detect any failure in the supply of gold by any test
I could apply—it follows irresistibly that the quantity
of gold in England ought never to have caused the
slightest anxiety to English bankers. Nevertheless,
the feeling abides ; and one of its worst consequences
is that it blinds the eyes of bankers, and, by their
means, those of the commercial world, to the truth,
that a bank derives as much strength from the
deposit of a cheque as from a deposit of gold. A
ship arrives from Australia with 100,000*l.* worth of
wool and 100,000*l.* in gold. ˙ The gold is at once
lodged at the bank ; the wool is sold, and a cheque
for the proceeds is equally passed on to the ledger of
the bank. By what legerdemain of words can it be
pretended that the bank has not received 200,000*l.* ?
or that the cheque of the wool-merchant has not
been as valuable as the deposit of the gold ? It is
true that the cheque for the wool has never been
paid in money, but has been settled at the clearing-
house ; but without that cheque the balance against
the banker at the clearing-house would have been
100,000*l.* heavier. His resources are strengthened to
identically the same extent by the wool as by the
gold. But now observe the difference to the national
wealth. The gold comes to a country already fully
supplied with this metal. It has enough for all its
wants ; it possesses a sovereign for every purpose for
which it can use a sovereign. The payment of goods
given to the Australian for the metal is a national
loss, till that same metal can be exported to some
other country in exchange for commodities which

can be used and can act as wealth. The contrast
exhibited by the wool is complete. It is a useful
article: it can serve as capital, and afterwards pass
into consumption. The goods paid to the Australian
for the wool form the most direct and the most legitimate act of trade: they are exchanged for other
goods, for wool, and this is the essence of all trade.
The importation of the wool benefits every one all
round: it provides materials for our factories, capital
for our traders, wealth for the community. The importation of the gold is a national loss till it is re-
exported: the arrival of the wool is an event full of
benefit for traders, for the banker, and for the nation.

But I hear the reply which has so often met my
ears: 'It is all very fine for philosophers to talk
against the importance we attach to gold, but we
stand on a plain fact; we know from experience that
a bank which acquires more gold can and does lend
more. Here is the gold: the bank has it: it is the
thing we want: what folly, then, to deny that the
bank can afford us larger accommodation.' I, too,
will take my stand on a fact; and I commend it to
the careful study of these practical men. We are
told that the Bank of France has nearly fifty millions
of English pounds in its treasury. This money is
idle: it produces nothing to the Bank of France:
the Bank has every possible motive to turn this
money to account, and to earn a profit out of its
employment. But there it obstinately remains. The
directors are powerless for getting it out: it refuses to
be lent: it will not leave the Bank's cellar. In vain
may one exclaim that there are thousands of persons
eager to borrow, and that the Bank will only be too
glad to make advances with it: it does not stir, and

why ? Plainly, because, in the actual circumstances of
France, that gold is a useless metal—as useless, as
incapable of being turned to any advantageous account as an excessive stock of sugar or timber. The
wants of the country for napoleons in its daily
transactions is fully supplied : no efforts of the Bank
can place this superfluous coin in the pockets or tills
of Frenchmen. Now this being so, what would be
the feeling of the directors of the Bank of France
if an additional million were brought to them from
California ? Would they commence the business of
the day with the conviction that they had a million
more to lend ? Would they look forward to making
larger loans on discount, to reaping augmented profit ?
Would the men who closed yesterday with fifty millions
unlent have any feeling that they would do more
business to day with fifty-one ? The state of the Bank
of England at this hour is quite analogous with that
of the Bank of France : they are both hopelessly
gorged with gold. And yet there are writers who
dwell on the state of the bullion, who carefully note
the sums taken to the Bank, who try to explain any
variations in the ease or difficulty of obtaining advances by the magical effect produced, not on the
state of commerce as requiring more or less accommodation, but on the mercantile mind, by the addition
or removal of a few extra ingots from vaults already
crammed to repletion. And this is what they call
commercial experience, knowledge of the laws of
trade, orthodox opinions about currency, mercantile
intelligence. They seldom venture to call it science :
there lurks about them an unavowed consciousness
that this sort of thing is not exactly science, that
there is a lack of investigation of first principles,

an absence of patient and accurate analysis, in this
manner of writing, very different from the methods
of real science.

The condition of the bullion in the Banks of
France and England is a crushing fact for those
who are unable to reason, but can understand
only what may be seen and handled. The doctrine
that gold is the great object of trade is shipwrecked
on the vaults of these great banks; they show over-
whelmingly that gold-seeking merchants toil and
labour only to bury their beloved metal in the depths
of Threadneedle Street. There it lies accumulated,
pile upon pile: with what possible benefit to living
mortals, it is for writers of City articles to tell. As
yet, they have never revealed to the world the mystery
of their knowledge. I have never found one who
has attempted to explain the advantage of having
fifty millions of bullion, or who has connected this fact
with the belief of mercantile and City writers that
exchanges ought to be favourable, that gold ought
to be imported, that sums taken to the Bank ought
to be recorded as favourable signs for commerce, that
above all things the movements of this wonderful
metal ought to be watched. They will occasionally
regret that such enormous funds are not put to any
use; and they will take a plunge into moral philosophy to bring up some mental state, some over-
mastering emotion, some unaccountable despondency,
hard to explain on any commercial or psychological
principle, which sentences merchants to the doom of
Tantalus, and steps in to prevent the enjoyment
of the treasure which they have been exhorted to
accumulate. But to suspect that such a stock of
bullion is a waste, to challenge the theory about

the importance of taking gold to the Bank, to think whether they have any theory at all about the matter, are things which never occur to their imaginations.

But there is a second question which I desire to address to those who love favourable exchanges, and abhor what they call drains, and lay stress on the inflow of gold to the Bank. At Melbourne the exchange is always unfavourable: gold is always leaving Australia, and one never hears that the export works harm to that country. The view taken of an export of gold from Melbourne is radically different from that which is held respecting an export of gold from London. Whence comes this difference in the estimates placed on the same event in the two countries? Australia is a gold-producing land, we are told, and England is not. The answer is excellent: but it leads to further inquiry. Why is it good for a gold-producing country to export gold? No one can doubt that the reason is that it produces the metal in excess of its own wants: the surplus it sends away in exchange for other commodities which it requires. The perception of this fact prevents an export of gold from Melbourne from exciting the shudder which the same occurrence generates in London; but if there is to be any knowledge or science in the matter the analysis cannot stop here. We have still to ascertain what are those wants of gold in Australia, which are more than satisfied by her production of the metal, and which justify a judgment of approval on its export. And may not the same wants be equally satisfied in London, and may there not be a similar excess in England, equally calling for export? We cannot tell whether there

should be a different feeling as to the export of the
metal in the two countries, unless we know the
nature of the demand which exists for it in each
respectively. If we can learn what are the purposes
to which gold is applied in Australia, so as to ascertain when they are fully satisfied, we shall be able
to determine, in turn, whether England is or is not
under the same conditions. What, then, is the use
that Australia has for gold? Plainly this : it requires
sovereigns for that amount of buying and selling
which is carried out by the agency of sovereigns ;
and more sovereigns are produced than are needed
for this purpose. Every one therefore thinks it
natural that Australia should export sovereigns.
What, on the other hand, is the use that England has
for sovereigns? The same identically as Australia ;
and I affirm that since 1819, England has always
found herself in the same state as Australia, and
has been over-supplied with gold by trade, as Australia is by mining. From this fact—for I assert
it to be a fact, when judged by any legitimate test—
I deduce the conclusion that, as a rule, the export
of gold has been the right and desirable thing for
England, as for Australia. The fact, no doubt, is
fairly open to dispute. Gold certainly is not produced in England, and it is perfectly possible that
there may have been at times, nay, that there may
be always, a deficient supply. I may be in error in
asserting this fact ; but, at any rate, I do distinctly
state what are the purposes for which gold is demanded, and I add the proof that no one since 1819,
who wanted gold and could pay for it, ever was incapable of procuring it. On the other side, I challenge
those who hail with satisfaction the inflow of gold

into England, and never conceive of an export of gold
as being mischievous for Australia, to tell the world
plainly what is the measure by which they determine
that Melbourne always has too much and London too
little gold, and to refute me on a direct issue of fact
or principle, when I affirm that English trade constantly over-supplies England with gold. The difference of rule applied to Australia and to England
calls for explanation: I have given mine; if the
City and the writers of City articles pretend to knowledge on this matter, they are bound to give theirs.

One explanation, indeed, is frequently given in the
City; and it strikingly illustrates the knowledge of
Political Economy which prevails in that region.
The bullion, we are told, is represented by notes;
and that answer is held to dispose of the question.
An astonishing answer, truly. It means that for all
the gold taken to the Bank, notes are issued to the
public; and it implies, that as there can never be too
many notes, it can never be aught but good to buy
gold which leads to notes. To have plenty of sovereigns and notes sums up mercantile feeling about
currency. Plenty of currency is plenty to buy with:
and what can man desire better? Thus it seems nothing strange that England should lose some twenty
millions of her wealth solely that she may be able
to put forth in London as many pieces of paper.
This is the grand mercantile philosophy of the nineteenth century. We have got so many more notes,
the traders feel: and if twenty millions' worth of
the capital of the nation has been lost, in order to
enable the Bank of England to give us these magical
promises to pay, what does it signify? The acquisition of the notes stops all further inquiry. Let the per-

petual stream run on for ever—a stream fed by the
sacrifice of England's wealth, in exchange for a metal
transferred from a mine to a cellar—so long as more
notes are obtained by its means. It may be true
that the Scotch note and the old Bank of England
note raised their heads as high as any modern note,
though unsustained by a vast substructure of metal,
and though they might be issued in unrestricted
numbers: they did not afford to the merchants of
that day the incomparable satisfaction which the
knowledge that there is so much gold at the Bank
gives to traders in our time. To that satisfaction I
must leave them. It is vain to argue with those for
whom the enormous purchase of a metal for which
no possible use can be found is a matter of sentiment
and not of reason.

It remains that I should add a few words on exchanges. The term denotes the quantity of gold or
silver in the coin of one nation, as expressed in the
coin of another. When it is said that a sovereign
stands, when at par, at an exchange of 25 francs
and 20 centimes, the meaning of the expression is
that the gold contained in an English sovereign
possesses the same metallic value as the silver
contained in 25 French francs and 20 centimes. It
is obvious at once, that if all nations possessed a
common international coinage, so that the same coins
circulated everywhere, exchanges in the strict sense
of the word would cease to exist. French, Germans,
and English would all buy and sell with the same
identical money.

But there is a second meaning attached to exchanges which is quite independent of currency and
is full of interest to traders. Exchanges seldom stand

at par. English sovereigns are generally exchanged
against French napoleons or francs for a sum a little
greater or a little smaller than is required by the
exact value of the metal contained in the two
amounts exchanged. Exchanges are usually above
or below par; and the variations are of extreme
importance to merchants. These variations do not
arise from any currency cause, except in the case
of countries which use an inconvertible paper currency. The par of exchange between England and
France does not alter; because the quantity of gold
in the sovereign and the napoleon does not vary.
The exchange between America and England varies
from day to day, and sometimes very largely; because the exchange expresses the worth of greenbacks in gold, and the value of the greenbacks is
incessantly subject to fluctuation. But the variation
in the exchanges of which I am here speaking has
its origin in a totally different cause. It has no
connection with the intrinsic value of the coins, as
metals: it is a phenomenon of pure trade. It springs
from the settlement of the sales and purchases of
commodities made by two nations with each other;
and it would equally exist in all its force, if all
countries made use of the same coins. When France,
on any given day, has bought of England more than
England has bought of France, France is under the
necessity of paying the balance in a precious metal,
which we will suppose to be gold. How is that
gold to be paid to her creditors in England? France
may send napoleons: if so, they will incur cost
for freight and insurance; and when they arrive
in England, they will sell only for their worth as
metal, less a deduction which will be charged for

the cost of melting. The Frenchman, then, will have to send over more napoleons, more gold than is exactly equal to the amount of his debt. Under these circumstances he seeks out for some one who has a bill on England, that is, a bill which some one in England is bound to pay, and he will offer to the owner of that bill a premium, an additional sum beyond the quantity of gold implied by the number of sovereigns mentioned in the bill. He can afford to give such a premium, so long as it does not exceed the cost of actually sending over napoleons to England. Under such circumstances, the exchange rises above par : the sovereign is quoted at an exchange of 25. 30 ; and this exchange is said to be in favour of England.

It is plain that this fluctuation in the exchange, being dependent exclusively on the balance of payments to be made by the country which has bought more than it has sold, would not be extinguished by a universal international coinage. The Frenchman, in the case supposed, would always prefer to pay something extra for an order for giving sovereigns in England to paying the charges which would be incurred by an exportation of coin, whatever that coin might be. The interest which attaches to this fluctuation in the value of the same coin in the two countries would remain as unabated, as intense as ever. That interest is partly rational, and partly irrational. It is irrational, so far as it interprets the inflow of gold, the balance of payments in gold to England by the Frenchman, as a gain to England. It is irrational and in clear contempt of Political Economy, because it implies gross ignorance of the fact that gold, that currency, is a mean only and not

an end, and that it is taken in the sale of goods solely
to be parted with in the purchase of others. The
gold coming into England with a favourable exchange
is gold that is not wanted, and which imposes on the
Englishman the necessity of exporting it again, in
order to obtain something which he really requires.

But there is a mercantile interest attached to variations in the exchanges which is highly rational, and
which prescribes to the trader the duty of carefully
watching the causes which create these fluctuations.
A merchant who sees iron quoted at so many milreas
a ton in Brazil, and founds his calculation on the
milrea at its par value as a metal, and sends out a
cargo of English iron upon this understanding, might
find the venture to result in heavy loss, if when he
had acquired the milreas on the sale of the iron
he was able to procure only eighteen instead of
twenty-four or twenty-six English pence in exchange
for each of them. The causes which created this
difference would operate with equal energy if Brazil
used sovereigns and shillings instead of milreas ; for
those causes have no relation to currency or the intrinsic value of the coin, but solely to the necessity
of sending a balance of payment to England or the
reverse. The confusion of this legitimate and important interest attaching to the exchangeable value
of coin, whether the same or different, between two
countries with the unreal and unfounded importance
assigned to the import of gold implied by so-called
favourable exchanges, has worked much mischief in
impeding a right understanding of what in reality is
an extremely simple matter. It has misled even so
eminent a Political Economist as M. Wolowski. He
believes in the currency importance of favourable

exchanges, in their regulating influence over currency. But a favourable rate of exchange means absolutely nothing else than the fact that gold is coming into the country; and whatever value this fact may possess must consist in the effect produced by an increased supply of gold. That is a question which must be discussed by itself, apart from all reference to the exchanges: and I have already shown that England never is in want of gold, and never has therefore any motive for desiring, on the score of currency, any augmented supply of that metal.

I have now reached the end of the task which I had set myself to perform. I have stated to you what I believe to be the right explanation of the facts and principles of currency. My great object has been to show that the investigation contains nothing which is intricate or abstruse; nothing which forms an exception to ordinary laws, or requires any extraordinary powers of interpretation. The ideas of complexity, intricacy, and unintelligibleness have been but too generally associated with currency, and it has been my greatest aim to convince you that a complete exposition can be given of its nature and its laws with clearness and simplicity. I hope that on a review of the results which we have obtained you will see reason for thinking that my belief was not unfounded. You have seen that currency owes its origin to the division of labour, and to the consequent necessity of exchanging the products of each man's labour with those of others. Men living in civilized society have been obliged to select an intermediate commodity, for which every one should agree to give his own goods in exchange. That commodity, the metal of which coin is composed, is spontaneously taken by

every man in the sale of his goods, because the universal consent to accept it in exchange is a guarantee
to him that he shall be able to select at pleasure by
its means those particular commodities of which he is
in want. A sale for coin is thus seen to be half an
act; it is completed only when the coin has been
parted with, in turn, in the purchase of other goods.
Each sale thus becomes an act of barter, in which the
goods and the coin stand on absolutely equal terms,
and are exchanged as being equivalents—the intrinsic
value of the coin on one side, and of the articles
bought on the other, being the basis on which the
equivalents, the quantity of each to be exchanged,
are calculated. And since all goods sold are exchanged for the metal of the coin, in the proportion
of the cost of production of the metal and of the
goods severally, it comes to pass that the metal furnishes the means of comparing the values of all commodities with one another; for all have their prices
in coin affixed to them, and these prices are compared with one another. The quantity of this intermediate commodity that comes into actual use, the
number of the pieces of coin employed by society,
depends on the number of exchanges, the quantity of
buying and selling, in which the coin is actually
transferred from one hand to another. More than
that society cannot use. If more coin is produced,
it must be stored up in the lumber-room, or by being
depreciated, will be required in larger quantity
for the same work. A cheapening of coin has no
value in currency; it simply necessitates the use
of a larger quantity and a heavier weight for the
performance of the same work. The employment
of a reduced quantity of coin cannot carry on its

depreciation beyond its cost of production; in
that case, some of the mines would be abandoned.
Every sale is a barter for a metal — is a pre-
sumed exchange for coin; but it by no means
follows that the coin, though pledged or promised,
always actually passes from the buyer's hands to the
seller's. In an immeasurably larger proportion of
the exchanges carried out in a civilized country the
coin pledged in the purchase is never paid at all.
Every sale professes to give an equivalent of coin
for goods, but the actual payment in coin in
most sales is never made. The payment of the
coin pledged is effected by setting debts off against
each other; the final result being that one set of
goods is exchanged against another set of goods.
The calculation in money is a mere estimation; the
real payment is the exchange of the goods. Bills,
banknotes, cheques, and book-debts are the instruments by which these sets-off are made; the sellers
receive debts in payment, with which they acquire
other goods as effectually as with coin. The foreign
trade is carried on by bills, that is, by debts expressed
in a particular way; at home, most payments are
effected by transferring a debt due by a banker.

The perception that a good debt effected the work
of exchanging as well as the actual coin led to the
substitution of banknotes for a large portion of the
coin in circulation. Coin and notes are merely tools;
and their capacity to do their work, as of all tools,
depends on their quality. The goodness of coin, its
quality, the faculty it possesses of furnishing to a
seller who takes it a guarantee that he shall be
able to buy other commodities with it, consists in the
purity and weight of the metal of which it is com-

posed, that is, in its intrinsic value as a commodity
in the general market of the world. A banknote's
quality depends upon its being a good and safe debt—
a debt which can realize its profession to give
sovereigns on demand at the pleasure of its holder,
in other words, on its convertibility. It is by
being immediately convertible that a banknote gives
to a seller the guarantee he requires that he is
parting with his goods for a real equivalent. Banknotes are sound tools only so far as they are convertible ; and bankers accordingly keep reserves of
coin for paying their notes on demand. But as
bankers often fail in their business, the law in
England has stepped in with enactments for securing the payment of banknotes, and this interference with what otherwise might be considered a
private trade is grounded on the fact that banknotes
exercise a public function, and are accepted by the
public under a kind of semi-compulsion. The law
interferes with them, as it makes regulations for
passenger-ships, for cabs, for the transport of gunpowder and the like. The law gives a protection to
the public, which experience shows the public cannot
provide for itself.

The quantity of banknotes in circulation is subject
to the same rule as that which governs the quantity
of coin. It is regulated by the demand of the public ;
and that demand is determined by the quantity which
the public can find use for—that quantity which is
actually employed in making purchases and payments, including the reserves of bankers. It is the
public and not the issuers of notes, the buyers and
not the sellers of the tools, who fix how many shall
remain in circulation. The Mint and banks of

issue are mere shops for the sale of tools; and
exist under the same conditions as all other shops.
Provided that the public, when it wants and
can pay for a sovereign or a banknote, can procure this convenient tool, the quantity of sovereigns and banknotes in circulation has no importance, not a particle more of importance than the
number of umbrellas or steam-engines which are
at work in the world. An issuing bank has no
power of increasing its issues beyond the quantity
of notes required for practical use, for carrying in
one's pocket, for change in bankers' or tradesmen's
tills, for making actual and positive payments with.
Every attempt to put more into circulation will be
rendered abortive by the public immediately sending
back the excess to the bank for payment. And since
the vast multitude of payments are effected in England by other means than coin and banknotes, and
further, the bankers have no power of increasing
or controlling those issues which carry out only a
small part of the buying and selling of the country,
it follows that the view which attaches importance
to the state of the circulation, which attributes any
effects to it on trade, or prices, or rates of discount,
is built on an illusion, and involves a complete ignorance of the nature and functions of banknotes. The
quantity, moreover, of notes in circulation bears no
relation whatever to the amount of business transacted in the national trade, whether domestic or
foreign; for just as the foreign trade may be multiplied tenfold and yet be brought into equilibrium
by the same balance of gold at the end, so the
payments at home may be enormously increased
without requiring the aid of a single additional

P

sovereign or banknote. Bills and cheques and other machinery perform all the additional work. The quantity of notes or coin in circulation is related solely to those particular payments in which these tools are used; and the number of transactions employing these tools is more a matter of habit than of anything else. Ready-money payments would multiply their use; an extension of banking would diminish it.

A banker's power to grant loans to traders through the agency of notes is limited to those notes which the public retains in use and circulation. An issuing bank is practically a shop for the sale of particular tools: the public buys as many of these tools as it wants, and with the means thus supplied by the purchase of notes by the public, the bank can make advances to traders. In times of commercial difficulty, therefore, a bank can give no help by additional issues, except so far as the public buys at such times more notes and keeps them; but loans cannot be made to traders by increased issues, at the pleasure of the banker, because neither the borrowers nor those to whom they pay the borrowed notes have any increased use for notes, and do not keep them. A banker's resources are composed of debts lodged with him, which he transfers to other persons; these debts give command of capital, ability to purchase goods; but they are only legal claims and title-deeds, and in no sense money; and for all but an insignificant part, are never paid in money at all. We have thus arrived at the definition of a bank,—that it is an institution for the transfer of debts. Debts are the staple in which it deals, the resources of which it disposes, and the vital point is in no way how many sovereigns or banknotes are in circulation, but how much command of capital, how many debts have been lodged with bankers, and what power of buying they can thereby transfer to others. Hence the movements of the national wealth are the objects to study, and not whether gold is coming in or going out, or how many of the multitudinous payments of the nation are effected by the agency of coin or banknotes. In a word, sovereigns and banknotes are very useful tools, but they are also tools of very limited use. They serve to make exchanges of property; but there are other tools, such as bills, cheques and the like, which perform an immeasurably larger quantity of this work than sovereigns and notes.

The general result, then, which we obtain is that sovereigns and banknotes are commodities, contrivances, tools, which follow the same laws as all other commodities and tools, and have no special connection beyond any other tools with trade. The importance attached to them by the commercial world is an extravagance of the grossest kind. As articles sold and purchased in shops, the sole point of importance, as for all goods, is the goodness of their quality —that the sovereign is made of pure metal and has full weight, and that the banknote will be paid on demand. This matter of quality is a manufacturer's question, just as the best mode of making good cloth, and as such affords occasion for interesting discussion; but the quantity of these tools bought is the affair of consumers, and no more deserves being talked or written about than the number of pounds of tea or the quantity of hats sold by the grocers and the hatters. The perplexity, the confusion, the inextricable tangle which have so long and so cruelly beset currency have sprung up from one great taproot—the perverse importance attached to the quantities used of coin and banknotes. This has been the cause which has connected them with the money market, with the rates of discount, with financial occurrences, with the prosperity and adversity of trade ; and with the disappearance of this cause the natural simplicity of currency comes to light. The instruments of currency are ordinary commodities and nothing else.

Such is the view which I have formed to myself of the nature and principles of currency ; and I shall rejoice if it is as clear and simple to the minds of others as it is to my own.

APPENDICES.

APPENDIX I.

DRAINS AND RATES OF DISCOUNT.

IT is desirable to append a few more words in
explanation of a phenomenon which is undoubtedly of frequent occurrence. It is often seen that
an increased exportation of gold is accompanied by
what is called 'tightness' in the money market and
an augmented rate of discount; and from this fact
it is usual for City people to infer that the departure
of gold to foreign parts is the cause of the difficulty,
and of the dearness of the accommodation obtained
from bankers. The reasoning is erroneous, for it mis-
takes the effect for the cause. The gold withdrawn
from the Bank is not the parent of the rise in the rate
of its discount. The exportation of the gold is itself
the effect of another cause, the existence of a state
of trade, of engagements which necessitates a transmission of the metal abroad. If England has bought
from foreigners more than at the moment she has
sold to them, or if she has contracted to make a loan
of money to a foreign State, an exportation of
gold is inevitable, either to balance trade or to fulfil

the contract. The question then becomes, whether
the cause of the rise in the discount market is to
be sought in the injury produced by a diminished
supply of gold for domestic purposes in England,
or in the circumstances which have led to its exportation. I have shown in the Lectures, that
England always possesses more gold than she can
use, and that the application of no test has succeeded
in demonstrating any deficiency of supply since
1819: it is hopeless, therefore, to attempt to trace
the difficulty in the money market, whether light
or severe, to any action generated by a scarcity of
the metal. The mere fact of exportation will not
furnish the explanation which we are in search of.
Not the slightest effect would be produced on the
rate of discount and the facility of obtaining loans,
if, unknown to the public, the Directors of the Bank
of England sent away, as a foreign loan, three or four
of the millions kept in the vaults of the Issue
Department. The rise in the rates demanded for
loans comes from a totally different source. It is
the result of the position of the exporters of the
gold and of the manner in which they act. An
excess of imports over exports, generating a demand
for metal to restore the equilibrium between purchases and sales abroad, generally implies that
these purchasers of foreign goods buy with the
means which they possess at their bankers. It is
the same with those who subscribe to foreign loans.
In the first instance, these loans are almost always
made out of funds lying at banks. In both cases,
demands are made on the resources of bankers;
either cheques are drawn on funds deposited with
bankers, or more commonly yet, advances are

asked of bankers. The number of borrowers from
banks increases; there are larger applications for
advances or discounts; and manifestly this is
a state of things which enables the bankers to
charge more for loans. The gold, as gold, has no
part in the matter. The borrowing and the drawing out of deposits from banks at the same moment
diminishes their resources and multiplies the applications for loans and discounts, and these are the
causes which raise the rate of interest, and render
the money market less easy.

The same identical effect would be produced if the
contract were to supply yarns or any other English
goods instead of gold. The applications for advances
from banks would pour in with the same urgency;
the same accommodation, the same lending would be
asked for, and the same rise in the rate of discount
would take place. And it is evident further, that
the effect would be equally great, whether the gold
exported came from a large or small stock at home;
for the cause at work is not the gold itself, not the
article actually sent abroad, but the demand made
on the resources of the loan market in order to purchase that article, be it gold, yarn, or any other
commodity. There is not a tittle of proof to show that
any deficiency of the supply of gold in England has
ever since 1819 been created by what is called a foreign
drain; that gold has been dearer at the shops of
the bullion-dealers, or that a single person has been
thereby inconvenienced by any difficulty to procure
a sovereign. The stock of gold in England, as in
Australia, has always been in such excess as to allow
of a large exportation of the metal without rendering
gold scarce in a single quarter. No man who had

a specific want for sovereigns has had to give a penny of premium to obtain them; no one has given a pound extra for a bag of sovereigns, as was so often given for a bag of shillings when silver coin was really scarce. A demand of a couple of millions of gold to pay for an excess of imports, or to make a loan to a foreign Government, would send up the rate of discount, whether the stock at the Bank was five or fifteen millions, because the export would be made at the cost of a diminution of the resources deposited at bankers, of their buying and lending power; but if the Bank itself lent the gold directly, was the true lender of the metal, no effect whatever would be produced on the money market. I have never heard of a large exportation of gold by the dealers in bullion leading to any aggravation of the money market; yet, if gold itself, the very metal, is the disturbing force, it must act equally wherever it exists in the country, whether it be in Threadneedle Street or in Cheapside. But it is quite true that a diminution of the gold at the Bank of England is often accompanied by a rise of discount; but the cause is not any deficiency of a useful commodity, but a demand for loans on the Bank for making payments abroad. An obligation to send two millions' worth of yarns as a balance of trade would produce precisely the same effect at the Bank of England: its resources would be drawn upon, and gold would equally leave its vaults. Only in the latter case, it would flow to the makers of yarns in England, and not being wanted for use by them, would be returned swiftly to the Bank's cellars. But the rise of discount would have been established.

Let me put a case in illustration of the preceding

analysis. Let us suppose that the Bank of England
has on one day thirty millions of deposits, that is,
owes thirty millions to its customers, and that it has
lent to trade twenty of these millions and possesses
the remaining ten in the shape of gold. On the
following day let us further suppose that these customers have drawn out four millions of their deposits
in gold. The Bank has now twenty-six millions of
deposits, and six millions of gold. But how much
has the money market? How much have traders
received either on the discount of bills or on advance?
Identically the very same amount as on the day preceding—twenty millions on each day alike. There
are four millions less in the vaults of the Bank, and
four millions less of deposits : the Bank's resources
are nominally lessened by four millions, but then
it is the idle, the unused, the temporarily annihilated
resources slumbering in the cellar which are lessened.
The gold is gone to pay for corn in America ; but
the resources of the Bank and of traders have not
been diminished a single pound by the operation.
How is it possible, in the face of such a fact, to assert
that the exportation, the drain of gold has exercised
a particle of action on the rate of discount ? Trade
has the same resources at its command on both days
alike : the same sum has been devoted to the discount office : the same amount of bills has been
accepted by the Bank, the same quantity of loans
granted : where is the point, I ask, at which the departure of the gold has made itself felt, and produced
the shadow of an effect on the money market ?

This argument compels me to infer that when
eminent writers like Mr. Tooke exhort the Bank to
check a drain by a rise of discount, they employ

language which is inaccurate and very apt to have mischievous consequences. They place the saddle on the wrong horse : they confound effect with cause. A drain of gold never produces harm, for there is always gold to spare in England : the thing to be checked and avoided is the getting into excessive debt abroad. If England is pledged to payments to foreign countries, there is nothing she can export with so little injury to herself as gold. A drain of gold to procure corn after a deficient harvest is an excellent event—one to be encouraged and not repressed ; and to tell bankers to try to avert it is to exhort them to starve the people. No doubt the rate of discount is very likely to be high whilst the exchange of gold for food is going on, but it will not be the departure of the gold but the loss of the wealth, consumed in the tillage of English fields and not replaced by the harvest, which will have rendered the nation poor, and diminished its capital, and multiplied applications to bankers for loans. Neither bankers nor merchants have the slightest interest, not only to procure back the gold exported abroad, but even to prevent it from taking wing to other lands ; for gold is not the thing which traders ask for, or bankers lend. As Sir John Lubbock's figures have already taught us, gold is not the article in which bankers deal : it is only their small change, nothing more.

But I shall be told that I overlook facts as they occur in real life. I shall be reminded that commercial crises always begin with a severe dimi- nution of banking reserves, with a heavy reduction of their stock of gold, with anxious agitation in banking minds how to meet demands for payment,

with distressing doubts as to the possibility of procuring sufficient gold to face engagements and avert
bankruptcy. Are not the eyes of the whole mercantile community fixed at such times on the bullion ?
and would not the Directors of the Bank feel un-
utterable relief if a million of Australian sovereigns
arrived at such a moment, and were lodged in the
reserves of the banking department ? How then can
I, in the teeth of such a fact, venture to assert that
gold is not the one important commodity, the one
specific remedy for these distressing evils ? I answer
that these facts are undeniable, and yet that they
do not furnish an iota of proof to show that a deficiency of gold has engendered the crisis, or
diminished the resources of bankers. A commercial
crisis is never an agony, a demand, for gold. It is
quite true that in former times, when the notes of
country bankers were open to just suspicion, a crisis,
as in 1825, directed a heavy demand for gold on many
banks of issue. This was a true, a specific demand
for gold ; but it was the child of distrust : it had no
root in any currency cause. Such demands have
now passed away : they have not been seen in modern
panics : they may be left totally out of account here.
On the other hand, an easy proof can be given that
a commercial crisis is not a demand for gold. If it
were so, the demand for the metal would make itself
felt at every bullion-dealer's shop all over England.
Who has ever heard that in 1847, or 1857, or 1866,
gold was eagerly bought from bullion-merchants at
advanced prices ? They may have been asked to
lend gold—that is possible, though I have never
seen any statement of such an occurrence ; but
that gold has been bought at such periods by

bankers and paid for out of their banking resources, is an event which has never happened;
and this is a complete demonstration that there
was no specific demand for the actual metal, gold.
The Australian sovereigns, if lodged with the Bank
as a deposit, would undoubtedly have multiplied
its resources; but a cheque for the same amount
on a sale of wool would have rendered the same
identical service. A bank pressed for repayment by
its depositors or its note-holders might find itself
compelled to sell its capital or any other property
in its possession; but this would not be a demand
for gold, for the sale would be made against cheques,
and its proceeds would be realized, not in metal, but
at the clearing-house.

In severe crises, no one denies it, the point at
which the pressure is felt is the reserves of bankers.
It is a want of gold in a particular place, and not
in the general market of the country, which creates
the anxiety; and its cause has its origin in the
nature of banking and not in currency. The peculiarity of a crisis is the failure of borrowers
to meet their engagements. Debts and loans are
not repaid; the bankers are involved in losses,
and are exposed, in addition, to unexpected claims
for repayment from depositors driven on by wild
feelings of alarm and distrust. Their reserves
dwindle rapidly away, for they are unable to call
in their means from those to whom they lent them
as quickly as the demands of their creditors for
repayment pour in upon them. This is a danger
inherent in the business of banking, and it should
be the perpetual study of every banker to keep it
ever in view, and so to lend as still to be able to

recall his loans as fast as he is summoned to repay
those which his customers have made to him. But
gold plays no part in this matter. If the banker's
loans are not repaid as rapidly as he pays the
cheques of his depositors, no purchase of gold can
help him: nothing but a loan of gold could be
of any benefit; and the loan of a cheque would
strengthen his reserve just as effectually. A banker
has no interest to receive payment of a cheque given
to him in metal rather than at the clearing-house:
his reserve is equally strengthened in either case.
The rapid diminution of the reserve indicates, not
that gold is deficient in the country, but that the
banking is going wrong; that its primary condition
is failing; that the equilibrium between receipts
and lendings is disappearing; that the banking
machinery is out of order. If the banking was
sound, and the difficulty lay in a specific need of
gold, the banker could at once make himself straight
by buying gold at the nearest bullion-shop; but,
on the other hand, if the banking is unsound, if he
cannot call in his loans as swiftly as he is forced
to pay his debts, nothing can help him except the
sale of his capital or property, or else free loans
granted to him by others, and this is a resource
which, from the nature of the case, always fails him
in times of panic and crises.

A rise, then, in the rate of discount is not an
event of currency; it is an occurrence of pure banking alone. It is the result of an excess of demands
over receipts at the banking-houses; and we have
seen that bankers deal in debts; that their means
are composed of debts; that what they receive and
transfer are debts. Writers on currency, however able,

work much mischief by directing the eyes of bankers
to their small change, to the supply of gold in the
country, for they turn their thoughts away from the
perception that the true thing to watch is the increase
or diminution of capital, that is, of material wealth.
It is by the growth of capital that the resources of
bankers become larger, and by its diminution that
they tend to dwindle away. But the machinery of
distribution smothers the facts which underlie it :
the ledgers, the cheques and bills, the list of prices
at the Stock Exchange, rates of discount and states
of the circulation, hide from view the wealth which
they neither create nor handle; with which they have
no other concern than to distribute its ownership.
When commodities are increased, when more is produced in the nation, sales multiply, and savings are
apt to be accumulated, and out of these savings
additional means flow in to bankers. But how are
these savings effected? Where and in what form
do they exist? Where are they to be found, so that
we may be able to put our fingers upon them? Let
us examine a particular case : *ex uno disce omnes.*
A landowner finds that his rents have risen, and
that his income has exceeded his expenditure. He
may consume the excess in keeping additional
hunters, or enlarging his mansion, or in some other
form of unproductive consumption. There will be no
saving for the country in that case, and no increase of
resources for the money market. But he may decide
to save instead of enlarging his consumption. The
difference in the facts will then be this. He has received a larger share of sheep and corn grown upon
his farms, and he has not consumed them unproductively, either directly within his own house, or

indirectly by destroying a larger quantity of other commodities, which he has bought with these sheep and corn bags. This increase of production remains in the nation as saving, as capital. It is sold by the tenant : it is paid for with a cheque : this cheque is passed on to the landlord's banker, and bestows upon him a purchasing power which it is his trade to transfer to others. A buyer has now the possession of the sheep and corn ; they constitute the saving : it is these sheep and corn which owe the debt lodged with the banker. The landlord is the real owner of this debt, and so long as he leaves it with the banker, he is remunerated by the satisfaction of having a larger balance at his banker's, or else by a certain amount of interest allowed him by the banker. We thus discover how it happens that the money market has more to lend, and that the rate of discount becomes easier : but what has the supply of gold to say to the matter ?

A similar analysis will explain a point almost universally misunderstood. We hear much of the prostration which follows a great commercial crisis, of the subsequent collapse of confidence, of the indisposition to undertake new enterprises, of a paralysis of trade. These effects are referred to some mood of mind, which has suddenly over-taken traders ; a feeling akin to the disgust which comes over losers at a gambling table. But if the crisis had produced no other effect than to transfer money, as in a bet, from one pocket to another, it would have been no crisis at all : trade would have remained undisturbed. If the fall of the great house of Overend had meant nothing more than the rise of another huge bill-brokering establishment

on its ruins, the money market would have sustained
no shock, the supply of means at bankers' would not
have been altered. But a commercial crisis has a far
different significance: its convulsions proceed from
a volcano, not of credit, but of wealth. Credit,
the willingness to lend, the ability to borrow, no
doubt, are vastly impaired by a crisis; but it is
not the cause of its disasters. A true crisis is a
destruction of means, a diminution of wealth; that,
and that alone, can have any importance. We know
that thousands of persons have been ruined by the
calamities of 1866; that new undertakings cannot be
launched, because the public is too poor to take up
shares; that the making of railways has all but
ceased in England; that ruin has been widely spread
by the failure of banks and public companies. But
have the losses of some been the gain of others?
Have as many men been made rich as have been
impoverished? Manifestly this is not the truth of
what has happened: the poverty is real, the public
wealth has been lessened. The downfalls of the City
have been produced by the destruction of the foundation of substance beneath. Wealth has perished;
how did it disappear? In unproductive consumption
of the food, clothing, and tools of labourers who
produced nothing in return, in pulling down and
building up houses in foreign countries, in the construction of public improvements, in opening unproductive mines, in the loss of the wealth formerly
supplied to us by the growers of cotton in America,
in the diminution of the American trade, in capital
sent from England to extend the cultivation of
cotton in India, Egypt, and the colonies. These,
and other operations similar to these, have been the

processes by which commodities have been diminished, and the stock of capital, of wealth, reduced; and these have been the abysses which have swallowed up the national resources, and brought great City firms to the ground. Public companies, no doubt, encouraged and extended this destruction of property; but, ultimately, it was not the companies but the labourers, the consumers of food and tools, which actually annihilated the wealth.

With such facts before our eyes, is it difficult to understand that the national recovery should be slow? It is the poverty and not the temper of the public which retards the restoration of trade to its former dimensions. The lost capital must be replaced, and that can be effected by savings only—savings of goods produced and not consumed unproductively. Writers of City articles hail the arrivals of gold to England; but they only impede the recovery. The purchase with the national wealth of a metal which is not applied to any useful purpose cannot increase that wealth. The more gold that England buys and retains, the less return does she obtain for the articles destroyed in the manufacture of the goods wherewith she bought the gold, the more she consumes unproductively. There is no possible escape from this conclusion. The City writers must either tell the world categorically what is the specific return which the gold makes for the cost of its purchase, or they must construct a new science of Political Economy of their own.

APPENDIX II.

LETTER FROM M. MICHEL CHEVALIER,

Senator, and Member of the Institute of France.

— · —

Paris le 8 Janvier 1869.

Mon cher Collègue,

Vous me demandez un exposé succinct de la manière dont s'est fait le Traité de Commerce entre les deux grands pays de l'Occident de l'Europe : je m'empresse de vous satisfaire.

L'origine du Traité de Commerce entre la France et l'Angleterre remonte à l'Exposition de 1855. Cette solennité démontra que l'industrie Française était fort habile et qu'il n'y avait pas de prétexte à la protéger par la voie de la prohibition absolue, ou par des droits exorbitants. Le Gouvernement, en conséquence, présenta au Corps Législatif, pendant la session de 1856, un projet de loi portant la levée des prohibitions. On se rappelle que depuis la loi du 10 brumaire an V, la prohibition était appliquée à la presque totalité des objets manufacturés. Le Corps Législatif, si souple ordinairement, fit un accueil brutal au projet de loi. Le Gouvernement, tout-puissant qu'il était, dut céder et le retirer ; il se crut même obligé de prendre, par une note insérée au *Moniteur*, l'engagement de ne pas lever les prohibitions avant cinq ans. J'avais eu connaissance, comme Conseiller d'État, de l'hostilité du Corps Législatif, car c'était le Conseil d'État qui était l'intermédiaire entre le Gouvernement et le Corps Législatif, et les prétentions de ce dernier avaient été discutées en Conseil d'État. Une de ces prétentions était que le Gouvernement Impérial, quand on aurait levé les prohibitions, fût dépouillé de la faculté, qu'il tenait de la constitution de l'Empire, de négocier des traités de commerce avec des changements de tarif, sans que ces changements de tarif eussent besoin d'être sanctionnés par le pouvoir Législatif. Je fus convaincu dès lors qu'on ne pourrait arriver à la réforme douanière et s'acheminer vers la liberté du commerce qu'en se servant précisement de ce pouvoir, reconnu à l'Empereur par la constitution, de faire des traités de commerce sans avoir besoin d'en faire sanctionner les clauses par le Corps Législatif. Dans cette situation d'esprit, j'attendis qu'une occasion favorable se présentât.

Pendant cette même exposition de 1855, où j'étais membre de la Commission Impériale et du Jury, je rédigeai une déclaration qui fut signée par un grand nombre de jurés et de commissaires de toutes les parties du monde, en faveur du système métrique. Sur cette base une société internationale fut constituée immédiatement pour la propagation de ce système de poids et mesures, et j'en fus un des présidents. On verra bientôt que cette société servit d'occasion aux démarches qui amenèrent le traité de commerce avec l'Angleterre.

Au commencement de 1859 Lord Palmerston, devenu chef du Gouvernement, offrit à Richard Cobden, alors en Amérique, un siège dans le cabinet, ce que celui-ci refusa péremptoirement dès son arrivée en Angleterre. Quoique n'ayant pas voulu être ministre, Richard Cobden n'en soutint pas moins avec ses amis le cabinet de Lord Palmerston contre le parti Tory. La majorité ministerielle étant faible dans le Parlement, le Ministère avait les plus grands égards pour le groupe de membres indépendants, appelés l'École de Manchester, dont Richard Cobden était le chef avec M. Bright.

A ce moment une négociation entre la France et l'Angleterre, pour un changement du tarif des douanes françaises, et la modification des articles du tarif Anglais concernant certaines productions importantes de la France, se présentait comme ayant des chances favorables par le concours qu'y donnait l'intérêt politique des deux gouvernements. Le cabinet dirigé par Lord Palmerston devait, s'il faisait un traité pareil, s'attacher les représentants des villes manufacturières, et renforcer d'autant sa majorité qui en avait grand besoin. De son côté l'Empereur Napoléon III craignait le renversement de Lord Palmerston, chez lequel il trouvait, dans ce temps-là, des dispositions amicales, tandis que le parti Tory lui montrait des sentimens hostiles. Il devait donc être bien aise de donner des forces à Lord Palmerston, indépendamment de ce qu'il ne pouvait que lui convenir d'élargir en Angleterre le débouché de l'industrie française et de débarrasser la France de l'entrave des prohibitions et des droits prohibitifs, car il était sympathique à la liberté du commerce. Il avait suivi avec attention, pendant son exil en Angleterre, les conférences de la Ligue.

M'étant rendu en Angleterre dans l'été de 1859 pour passer quelque temps chez un de mes amis, j'avais revu à Londres Richard Cobden, avec lequel j'étais lié depuis le voyage que celui-ci avait fait en France en 1846, et je l'avais mis au courant de la disposition relative aux traités de commerce qui existe dans la constitution de l'Empire. Je lui avais démontré la convenance et la légitimité en principe d'un traité de commerce entre la France et l'Angleterre, dans le but de resserrer les liens entre les deux pays par le moyen d'un traité qui accomplirait la réforme douanière de la France. Je lui avais fait comprendre qu'une telle réforme, quelque avantageuse qu'elle fût, était absolument impraticable par le procédé d'une loi délibérée au Corps Législatif, à cause des préjugés, excités jusques à la violence, qui existaient dans cette assemblée.

Richard Cobden avait résisté d'abord à l'idée d'un traité de commerce, en alléguant que c'était contraire au principe de la liberté commerciale, puisqu'il faudrait, disait-il, que par ce traité l'Angleterre prît envers la France des engagemens particuliers, tandis que, sur le terrain où elle s'était placée en accomplissant sa réforme douanière de 1846, il

lui était commandé désormais de traiter toutes les nations
de la même manière. Mais il vit bientôt que le traité pourrait
être rédigé de telle sorte que l'Angleterre modifiât, en faveur
de tous les peuples sans exception, son tarif sur les points
qui intéressaient la France, tandis que la France se bornerait
à faire des réductions de tarif en faveur de la seule Angleterre.
Une fois d'accord sur ce point nous nous séparâmes, et Richard
Cobden prépara le terrain par ses entretiens avec les membres
du Gouvernement.

Au mois d'octobre de la même année, je revins en Angleterre en profitant de l'occasion que m'offrait le congrès
international des poids et mesures qui se réunissait à Bradford
et à la présidence duquel j'avais été appelé. En réalité
l'objet principal de mon voyage était le traité de commerce.
J'arrivai à Londres le 8 et dès le lendemain je me concertai
avec Richard Cobden, qui m'attendait, puis je partis pour
Bradford en compagnie de M. Benjamin Smith, de la Chambre
des Communes, ami particulier de Cobden et l'un des plus
anciens champions de la liberté commerciale. De là j'allai
voir à Rochdale M. Bright auquel j'avais été annoncé. Celui-ci
me déclara explicitement qu'il adhérait sans réserve à la
combinaison du traité de commerce, et m'encouragea à
travailler pour la cause que, dans sa conviction chaleureuse,
il appelait *la foi*. Ce fut le terme dont il se servit quand
nous nous séparâmes. Je revins à Bradford pour la réunion
des poids et mesures, j'achevai ce que j'y avais à faire, et le
14 je partis pour Londres, où M. Cobden avait admirablement
employé son temps.

M. de Persigny, ambassadeur de France à Londres, avait
été mis par moi dans la confidence de ce que je préparais
avec M. Cobden, et il avait usé de son influence personnelle
dans le même sens. Il s'était prononcé déjà en France, quand
il était ministre, pour une réforme profonde du tarif des
douanes, et avait pris part aux changements accomplis par
décret à titre provisoire.

J'eus une conversation avec M. Gladstone, Chancelier de
l'échiquier, le 15 au soir, après la réunion du cabinet. C'était
un samedi. Je lui fis connaître la disposition inscrite dans

la constitution de l'Empire et la latitude qu'avait ainsi
l'Empereur pour négocier des traités de commerce. D'ailleurs
je ne lui dissimulai pas que je n'avais aucun pouvoir pour
traiter; mais j'ajoutai que, d'après certaines circonstances,
j'avais tout lieu de penser que l'Empereur accueillerait
favorablement l'idée d'un traité largement conçu, surtout si
ce traité abolissait les droits encore élevés qui frappaient une
importante industrie de la France, celle des soieries, ainsi que
les articles fabriqués en peau, et un assez grand nombre
d'articles compris sous la dénomination générique *d'articles de
Paris*, et si enfin il devait en résulter une forte réduction du
droit énorme établi sur les vins. On sait que ce droit était de
près de 6 shillings par gallon, ou de 1 f. 60c. par litre. M. Gladstone répondit que l'Angleterre abolirait les droits sur tous les
articles manufacturés à Paris et à Lyon, et spécialement sur
les soieries, la ganterie, les chaussures, les modes, les articles
spécialement dits *de Paris* en général, et réduirait le droit
sur les vins, du point où ils étaient d'environ six shillings
par gallon, à deux shillings.

En trois quarts d'heure tout fut convenu entre le Chancelier
de l'Échiquier et moi. Les dispositions sur lesquelles nous
fûmes d'accord furent à peu près celles que porte le traité
de commerce définitivement signé le 23 janvier 1860.

En quittant M. Gladstone, j'allai rejoindre Cobden qui
m'attendait au club de *l'Athenæum*. Nous nous félicitâmes
de la tournure favorable que prenait le projet, et nous nous
donnâmes rendez-vous à Paris où nous convînmes d'arriver
séparément, afin de ne pas donner l'éveil aux prohibitionistes
qui, s'ils eussent soupçonné ce dont il s'agissait, auraient fait
une levée de boucliers et mis le Gouvernement dans l'im-
possibilité d'accomplir une réforme pourtant si nécessaire.

Richard Cobden, qui avait sa famille à Brighton, y passa
quelques jours. Moi, je pris la voie directe de Folkstone et
Boulogne. Nous nous retrouvâmes ainsi le 22. L'Empereur
fut averti par M. Rouher, auquel j'étais allé, aussitôt à Paris,
dire ce que j'avais fait, et que j'avais mis en relations avec
Richard Cobden. Il nous reçut à Saint Cloud le jeudi, mais
isolément. Il nous dit qu'il adhérait au projet du traité de

commerce et nous recommanda le secret pour quelques
semaines. Les négociations commencèrent quand l'Empereur
fut revenu de Compiègne, au milieu de novembre. Les né-
gociateurs furent du côté de la France : M. Rouher, ministre
du commerce, et M. Baroche, ministre des affaires étrangères
par *interim*, en replacement de M. Thouvenel, alors éloigné de
Paris ; du côté de l'Angleterre M. Cobden et Lord Cowley.
J'assistais et prenais part aux conférences. M. Achille Fould,
Ministre d'État, qui était prononcé pour le traité, entretenait
de tout son pouvoir dans des dispositions favorables l'Empereur,
qui du reste avait pris son parti. Le Ministre des Finances,
M. Magne, ne fut pas mis dans le secret, non plus que le
Directeur-général des Douanes M. Gréterin qui était, de
même que M. Magne, pour le système restrictif. Avant la
fin de décembre le traité était achevé ; mais le temps nécessaire
aux formalités diplomatiques a fait qu'il porte la date du 23
janvier suivant.

Le secret recommandé par l'Empereur fut bien gardé par
tout le monde. Je puis citer à ce sujet le détail suivant :
M. Rouher se méfiait de ses bureaux où la direction du commerce extérieure était confiée à un homme, fort honorable
assurément, mais partisan déclaré de la prohibition, et lié avec
les chefs prohibitionistes. Les bureaux du ministère ignoraient
donc complètement le travail auquel se livraient les ministres.
Les notes de M. Rouher étaient copiées par Madame Rouher,
de même celles de Richard Cobden étaient mises au net par
Madame Michel Chevalier. Quand les termes du traité
furent à peu près déterminés, l'Empereur révéla l'affaire
au conseil des ministres, où beaucoup d'objections furent élevées.
Les notabilités prohibitionistes averties accoururent à Paris.
L'Empereur et les ministres, M. Rouher surtout, furent as-
siégés. Mais rien n'ébranla la résolution du Gouvernement,
et le traité fut signé.

Le nom de la liberté du commerce n'y est pas prononcé,
non plus que dans les rapports et documents relatifs à l'affaire.
Mais la part que Richard Cobden et moi y avions prise fut
pour tout le monde, et surtout pour les prohibitionistes, la
preuve que la liberté du commerce était le but qu'on pour-

suivait. Les ministres dans leurs conversations ne le con-
testaient pas. Il faut pourtant dire, d'après des actes récents,
que le zèle du Gouvernement Impérial pour la liberté commerciale paraît assez attiédi. Est-ce un simple accident de
la politique, est-ce un revirement? C'est ce que dira l'avenir.

MICHEL CHEVALIER.

(*TRANSLATION.*)

My dear Colleague,

You ask of me a succinct statement of the manner in which
the Treaty of Commerce between the two great nations of the
West was made: I hasten to comply with your wish.

The origin of the Treaty of Commerce between France and
England dates from the Exhibition of 1855. That great public
event proved that French industry was exceedingly skilful,
and that there existed no pretext for protecting it, either by
absolute prohibition or by exorbitant duties. The Government, in consequence, presented a Bill for the repeal of Prohibition to the Corps Législatif in the session of 1856. It
will be remembered that since the law of the Tenth Brumaire,
Year V., well-nigh the totality of manufactured products had
fallen under the ban of prohibition. The Corps Législatif,
generally so submissive, gave a violent reception to the bill.
The Government, in spite of its overwhelming power, was
forced to yield and to withdraw the measure, and it even
felt itself compelled to give an assurance, by a note inserted
in the *Moniteur*, that it would not raise the Prohibition
before the end of five years. I had become acquainted, as
a member of the Conseil d'État, with the hostility of the
Corps Législatif, for the Conseil d'État was the medium between the Government and the Corps Législatif, and the
demands of this body had been discussed in the Conseil
d'État. One of these demands required, that after the aboli-
tion of prohibition the Imperial Government should be

deprived of the power bestowed upon it by the Constitution of the Empire to negotiate Treaties of Commerce, involving changes of tariffs without the sanction of the Corps Législatif. I became immediately convinced that it would be impossible to obtain a reform of the Customs or to make any progress towards Free Trade in any other way than precisely by making use of this power, which the Constitution recognized as belonging to the Emperor, of making Treaties of Commerce without the necessity of submitting their clauses to the sanction of the Corps Législatif. In this state of mind I watched for the arrival of a favourable opportunity.

During this same Exhibition of 1855, in which I was a member of the Imperial Commission and of the Jury, I drew up a declaration in favour of the Metrical System, which was signed by a great number of Jurors and Commissioners from all parts of the world. An international society was immediately instituted on this basis for the spread of this system of Weights and Measures, and I was one of its Presidents. It will appear presently that this society led to the steps which resulted in the Treaty of Commerce between France and England.

At the commencement of the year 1859, Lord Palmerston, who had become Prime Minister, offered a seat in the Cabinet to Richard Cobden, who was then in America, but which the latter declined as soon as he arrived in England. Although he did not wish to become a Minister, Richard Cobden did not the less on that account support along with his friends the Government of Lord Palmerston against the Tory party. The ministerial majority was weak in Parliament, and the Minister showed the greatest consideration for the group of independent members who were called the Manchester School, and were led by Richard Cobden and Mr. Bright.

At this period it was thought that the political interests of the two Governments of France and England combined to offer favourable chances of success for a negotiation between these two countries for a change in the French Customs and a modification of articles in the English tariff which related to certain important products of France. The Cabinet of which Lord Palmerston was the chief, by making such

a Treaty, would win the attachment of the representatives of
the manufacturing towns, and so far strengthen its majority
with a support which it greatly needed. On the other side,
the Emperor Napoleon dreaded the fall of Lord Palmerston,
who at that time entertained friendly feelings towards him,
while the Tory party cherished feelings of hostility. He
could not therefore help being very glad to give strength to
Lord Palmerston, independently of the fact that it could not
but be agreeable to him to extend the market for French products in England, and to rid France of the fetters of prohibition
and prohibitory duties ; for he had great sympathy with Free
Trade. During his exile in England, he had studied with
care the conferences of the League.

In the summer of 1859 I went to England to pay a length-
ened visit to one of my friends, and I met again in London
Richard Cobden, with whom I had become connected since
his journey to France in 1846. I informed him of the provision made in the Constitution of the Empire relative to
Treaties of Commerce. I showed him the propriety and the
legitimateness of a Treaty of Commerce between France and
England, which should aim at drawing closer the bonds
of union between the two countries, by means of a treaty
which should carry out a reform of the Customs in France.
I made him understand that such a reform, however beneficial
it might be, could not possibly be carried through by
means of a law submitted to the deliberations of the Corps
Législatif; for that assembly was under the dominion of pre-
judices that were pushed even to violence.

Richard Cobden opposed, at first, the proposal of a Treaty
of Commerce, on the ground that it was inconsistent with the
principle of commercial freedom—for, said he, it will be necessary for England in such a treaty to contract special engagements with France, and the principle on which her commercial legislature was based in 1846 bound her thenceforward
to treat all nations alike. But he soon saw that the treaty
might be so framed as to enable England to benefit all nations
without exception by a modification of her tariff on those
points which interested France, whilst France limited the

reduction of her duties to the advantage of England alone. As soon as we were agreed on this point we parted, and Richard Cobden prepared the way by communicating with the members of the Government.

In the month of October I returned to England, to take part in the International Congress on Weights and Measures which met at Bradford, and of which I had been invited to become the President. But the principal object of my visit was the Treaty of Commerce. I arrived in London on the 8th, and on the next morning I came to an understanding with Richard Cobden, who was waiting for me, and I then went to Bradford in the company of Mr. Benjamin Smith, M.P., who was a particular friend of Cobden, and one of the oldest friends of commercial freedom. Thence I went to pay a visit to Mr. Bright at Rochdale, who had been informed of my coming. He declared to me in explicit terms that he gave his unreserved adhesion to the Treaty of Commerce, and he urged me to work for the cause, which, in the warmth of his conviction, he called ' *The Faith.*' It was the expression he made use of when we parted. I returned to Bradford for the Meeting on Weights and Measures. I performed what I had to do in this matter; and on the 14th I set out for London, where Mr. Cobden had made an admirable use of his time.

I communicated to M. de Persigny, the Ambassador of France in London, the secret of what I was preparing with Mr. Cobden, and he employed his personal influence to the same end. He had already, when he was Minister, declared himself in France to be favourable to a thorough reform of the tariff, and he had taken part in those changes which had been effected by a Provisional Decree.

I had a conversation with the Chancellor of the Exchequer, Mr. Gladstone, on the evening of the 15th, after a meeting of the Cabinet. It was on a Saturday. I informed him of the power provided in the Constitution of the Empire, and of the liberty which consequently the Emperor possessed for negotiating Treaties of Commerce. However, I did not conceal from him that I had no power to treat; but I added that certain circumstances induced me to think that the Emperor

would receive with favour the proposal of a treaty, framed
in liberal terms, especially if that treaty were to abolish
the duties, all high, that were levied on an important
industry in France, that of silks, as well as on articles worked
in skins, and a somewhat large number of articles, comprised
under the generic designation of 'articles of Paris;' and
finally, if the result of the treaty were to be a strong
diminution of the duty levied upon wines. This duty
amounted to nearly six shillings a gallon, or one franc sixty
centimes per litre. Mr. Gladstone answered that England
would repeal the duties on all articles manufactured at Paris
and Lyons, especially on silks, gloves, shoes, and the articles
particularly described as 'articles of Paris,' and would reduce
the duty on wines from about six shillings, as it then stood,
to two.

Everything was settled between the Chancellor of the
Exchequer and me in three quarters of an hour. The arrangements on which we came to an agreement were nearly identical
with those which were contained in the definitive Treaty of
Commerce which was signed on January 23, 1860.

On leaving Mr. Gladstone, I went over to Mr. Cobden,
who was waiting for me at the Athenæum Club. We con-
gratulated each other on the favourable turn which our project
was taking. We arranged to meet in Paris, which we were
to travel to separately, in order not to attract the notice
of the Prohibitionists; for if they had suspected what was
going on, they would have ordered a levy of bucklers, and
would have prevented the Government from accomplishing
a reform which, nevertheless, was so urgently needed.

Richard Cobden then spent some time with his family at
Brighton. On my side, I took the direct road to Folkestone
and Boulogne. We met again on the 22nd. The Emperor
was made acquainted with the matter by M. Rouher, to whom
I had repaired immediately on my arrival at Paris to inform
him of what I had done, and whom I had placed in com-
munication with Richard Cobden. He received us at St.
Cloud on Thursday, but unattended. He told us that he gave
his adhesion to the Treaty of Commerce, and begged us to

keep the secret for some weeks. The negotiation began when the Emperor returned from Compiègne, in the middle of November. The negotiators were, on the side of France, M. Rouher, Minister of Commerce, and M. Baroche, Minister of Foreign Affairs, provisionally, in the absence of M. Thouvenel who was at a distance from Paris; on the side of England, Mr. Cobden and Lord Cowley. I was present at and took part in the conferences. The Minister of State, M. Achille Fould, had declared in favour of the Treaty, and to the utmost of his ability, kept up the good-will of the Emperor, who, indeed, had already made up his mind. Neither the Minister of Finance, M. Magne, nor the Director-General of the Customs, M. Grélerin, were made acquainted with the secret; they were both in favour of the Protective System. Before the end of December the Treaty was completed; but the time required for diplomatic formalities caused it to bear the date of the 23rd of the following January.

The silence recommended by the Emperor was well kept by all. On this point, I may mention the following circumstance. M. Rouher distrusted the officials of his department, in which the direction of Foreign Trade was in the hands of a man, who was assuredly most honourable, but was a declared partisan of the Prohibitive System, and was connected with the Prohibition leaders. The officials of the Government were completely ignorant of the business on which the Ministers were engaged. The notes of M. Rouher were copied by Madame Rouher; and in the same way those of Richard Cobden were written out fair by Madame Michel Chevalier. When the terms of the Treaty had been nearly settled, the Emperor revealed the affair to the Council of Ministers, when many objections were raised. The leaders of Prohibition, now informed of the danger, hurried to Paris; they besieged the Emperor and the Ministers, above all, M. Rouher. But nothing could shake the determination of the Government, and the Treaty was signed.

The name of Free Trade is not named in the Treaty, nor in the reports and documents relative to the affair. But the

part which Richard Cobden and I took in it was a proof for
all the world, and most of all for the Protectionists, that Free
Trade was the object that was pursued. The Ministers, in
private conversation, did not dispute the fact. It must be
remarked, however, that, judging from some recent acts, the
zeal of the Imperial Government in behalf of Free Trade
seems to have considerably cooled. Is this a simple accident
of politics, or a relapse? Time will show.

MICHEL CHEVALIER.

APPENDIX III.

I earnestly recommend a careful study of this excellent paper by Mr. Charles Gairdner, Manager of the Union Bank of Scotland at Glasgow. It is full of instruction. I do not quite agree with every statement it contains, as the readers of the Lectures will perceive; but the whole paper exhibits a precision of thought, a correctness of view, and a scientific treatment most rare amongst writers who belong to the commercial world.

Answers to certain of the Questions proposed by the Conseil Supérieur du Commerce de France on the subject of Banking and Currency.

On Paper Money.

16. *What is the utility of paper money?*

It is understood that the term 'paper money' is intended to include banknotes and any other forms of obligation, bearing no interest, and payable to bearer on demand.

Paper money has its origin and chief utility in its superior convenience as compared with the coin which it represents.

It has also an important utility in so far as by diminishing the quantity of coin in circulation it economises capital.

It confers a third advantage in respect that the amount of money in circulation in any country being a fluctuating quantity, an increase or diminution in the amount of paper money in circulation may take place without disturbing the stock of coin which forms the reserve.

17. *Is the part played by paper money tending to become very important?*

There is no particular tendency operating in Great Britain to make paper money more important.

18. *Is it by issues of notes payable to bearer at sight, or by means of transfers, current accounts, cheques, &c., that credit has a tendency to extend?*

It is not by issues of notes payable to bearer at sight, nor by any other form of obligation payable on demand, that credit has a tendency, to any appreciable degree, to extend.

The tendency of credit to extend arises mainly through the commitments of merchants, manufacturers, contractors, and others, the settlement or accomplishment of whose transactions is postponed.

19. *Can the employment of paper money take an indefinite extension? If not, in what limits shall it be confined?*

Paper money cannot take an indefinite extension. The amount of money (whether paper or coin) at any time in circulation is the aggregate amount contained *in the pockets and tills of the whole people.* This may be more or less according to circumstances; but as long as the paper is convertible into the coin which it represents, each individual will regulate for himself the amount retained for his own purposes; and it follows, that the aggregate amount in circulation is regulated by the requirements, or the convenience, or, it may be, the whims, of the community at large.

ON THE CONDITIONS OF A GOOD PAPER MONEY.

20. *Under what conditions does the employment of paper money present no inconveniences?*

The only condition that is at once essential and universal is that it be convertible into coin at the will of the holder. Other regulations may be required for the safety and convenience of particular communities, but these must be ascertained with reference to the circumstances of each case.

21. *Is the constant convertibility of notes indispensable ?*

Undoubtedly so.

22. *Does the unity of the banknote promote the circulation of it ?*

The unity of the banknote involves the supposition of there being only one bank of issue. This again of necessity involves that non-issuing banks shall keep a stock of notes procured from the single bank of issue. As this would not be necessary were all banks free to issue notes (as is the case with the existing banks in Scotland), it follows that the 'unity of the banknote' increases the *apparent* circulation by the amount of the note reserves of the non-issuing banks.

With this explanation, reference is made to answer 19 for the principle which regulates the amount of notes in circulation.

23. *What are the inconveniences and advantages of the plurality of banks, whether general or of limited circumscription ?*

This question appears to be in other words : 'What are the inconveniences and advantages of freedom as compared with monopoly ?'—for the non-plurality of banks *is* monopoly.

In reply, it may be stated that the arguments in favour of freedom in trade apply equally to freedom in banking ; and, further, that in England and Scotland the principle of freedom in banking is now all but universally accepted. A difference of opinion exists as to the propriety of allowing all banks to issue notes, but in Scotland the right to do so is regarded as an integral and important part of the business of banking.

The advantages conferred by the system of banking pursued in Scotland are seen—

(1) In the facilities afforded to the public by the establishment, throughout even the most remote districts, of branch banks. At present there are nearly seven hundred banking offices in Scotland, emanating from twelve parent banks.

(2) In the economy of capital so effected,—it being the universal practice of people even of the most moderate means to lodge their money with the banks. The cash deposits in Scotland approach sixty millions sterling. The population is about three millions.

(3) In the allowance of interest by the banks on all the money held by them from the public.

(4) In the advantages afforded to the industrious classes throughout the country by means of loans and advances.

(5) In the perfect security afforded to the public,—there never having been an instance of a joint-stock bank in Scotland failing to pay its debts in full; and the cases in which, in former times, the failure of a private bank involved loss were extremely rare.

(6) In the manner whereby, *through being free*, the banking institutions of the country have been able to adapt themselves to the changing circumstances of the country. The private banks, which formerly conducted a large proportion of the business of the country, had paid-up capitals of small amount, and a very limited number of partners. These have all now been absorbed into joint-stock banks, the amount of whose paid-up capitals varies from 100,000*l.* to 2,000,000*l.*, and each bank includes in its list of partners from 500 to 1500 individuals. In this way the security afforded to the public has kept pace with the demands of a constantly increasing commerce.

As opposed to these advantages, it is not known that there are any inconveniences to state arising out of the plurality of the banks.

On the Establishments which issue Paper Money.

26. *Is there advantage or inconvenience in separating the issue department from the discount department ?*

There does not appear to be any sound principle to justify the separation in question, and the experience of its working by the Bank of England has not proved it to be of any practical advantage, but, on the contrary, it has created on many occasions serious complications.

27. *If the notes of the Bank of France were made a legal tender, as is the case of those of the Bank of England, would it have the effect of promoting the circulation of them ?*

No. Refer to answers 19 and 22.

28. *What number of signatures ought a bank to require for its true security in the discount of bills ?*

Security is not to be ensured by the number of signatures to a bill, but by the exercise of a sound discretion as to the parties and the circumstances of each case.

29. *Ought the issue of notes to be limited ? Ought the issue to be proportionate to the metallic reserve of the capital ?*

(1) No,—referring to answers 19 and 22.

(2) It is not correct to say that the issue should be proportionate to the metallic reserve of the bank,—but rather that the metallic reserve ought to be proportionate to the *character* and *amount* of the liabilities of the bank, whether upon notes or upon other forms of obligation, and this is a mode of stating the case not sufficiently attended to and considered.

ON BANKING OPERATIONS.

30. *At what level ought to be maintained the metallic reserve of the Bank of France in order to secure the convertibility of the notes ?*

There is no fixed rule which can be stated in answer to this question. Every bank ought to know the character and amount of its own liabilities,—keeping constantly in view that the deposits equally with the notes are payable in coin, and that in times of pressure a demand for gold and silver is more likely to arise from a withdrawal of deposits than from a diminution of notes in circulation.

It is also to be kept in view that Paris and London are the natural bullion marts of France and England ; because, in Paris and in London the exchange operations with foreign countries are chiefly conducted. It follows that the banks in these cities (and notably the Bank of France and the Bank of England) hold the chief bullion reserves of all the banks in the two countries, and these reserves are accessible to any bank which holds the obligations of the bullion-holding banks.

The *character* therefore of the liabilities of banks in Paris and London differs essentially from that of the country banks—from whom coin or bullion, in large quantity, is seldom demanded,—and the metallic reserve that may be adequate and proper for the one forms no guide to that which is essential to the safety of the other.

31. *What are the causes which tend to reduce or augment the metallic reserve, and the means to be employed to maintain the level of it?*

The causes that affect the metallic reserve may be classed under three heads :—

(1) The natural increase or diminution of gold and silver coin in active circulation,—i. e. in the pockets and tills of the people.

(2) Hoarding. This may be either from ignorance or from want of confidence in the banks.

(3) Receipts from or payments to foreign countries.

The means capable of being employed by banks to counteract these influences, are as regards

(1) The issue of banknotes of such denomination as will meet the particular demand of the time. The prudence, however, of having recourse to this expedient must always be considered with reference to other circumstances besides the question of the metallic reserve.

(2) The removal of the causes of hoarding is so far as it may be possible to do so.

(3) The raising or depressing of the rates of interest and discount.

32. *What is the part played by, and the destination of, the capital of the bank? Ought the capital to be increased? What would be the effects of the increase?*

The capital of the bank is a fund contributed by those who are to enjoy the profits of the business, as a protection or guarantee to the creditors of the bank.

Assuming that the capital is sufficient in amount to secure entire confidence in the stability of the bank, there is no advantage to be gained by its being increased.

GLASGOW, 2nd *April*, 1866.

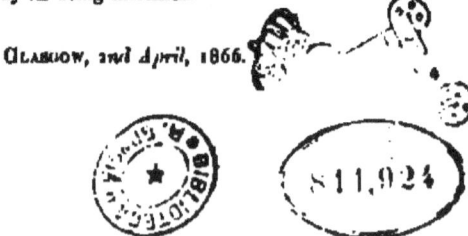

www.ingramcontent.com/pod-product-compliance
Lightning Source LLC
Chambersburg PA
CBHW020104030726
47498CB00006B/1934